**MINNETAKA
INDIAN BOY**

Bergquist Publishing
414 West Seventh Street
Willmar, Minnesota 56201
(612) 235-4516

First Edition, July, 1985
Copyright © 1985 J. Gordon Bergquist
All Rights Reserved

Library of Congress Number
85-072434

International Standard Book Number
0-9615483-0-4

J. GORDON BERGQUIST
AUTHOR/ARTIST

Other Books by J. Gordon Bergquist

Summer Boy
Once a Boy
(See Back Page For Order Form)

To my wife: *Janice*

CREDITS:

Mary Lou & Richard Arne
John Broberg
Edythe Langager
Jerome Miller
Thomas Miles
Vernon Thompson

FOREWORD

This is a work of fiction based upon general information about the history of the Dakotah (Sioux) and Chippewa (Ojibway) Indian Tribes of Minnesota. It is intended, therefore, to be an entertaining story, not a historical novel in the exact definition.

Because this story takes place before the coming of white men, it was necessary to change some place names of the area, mainly lakes and rivers, to make them sound natural. Some names have been retained; others are fictional. Thus, maps have been provided to make the narrative clear when reference is necessary.

It has been just recently that white men have studied objectively the culture of the original native, the American Indian. As a nation we have confessed to our cruel, inhumane, and systematic decimation of the hundreds of Indian nations. But confession, while commendable, cannot turn back the calendar.

In the ruthless killing and displacement of the Indian, we overlooked lessons that Indian culture could have taught us. The most notable of these lessons was their adaptation to their natural surroundings.

By contrast the white men, coming from a variety of nations, gobbled up chunks of territory whose size was in direct relation to the ability of their soldiers to enforce their tenuous hold on the new land.

Their settlers, while coming from many motherlands, had one characteristic in common. It was a name used to characterize everything American. The word was "Enterprise." As if the word didn't carry enough latitude in itself, common usage added "Free Enterprise." The exciting word was to inflame the dreams of the European peasant. He visualized his personal role in self rule, justice under laws of equality, and a freedom to worship. Gold, free land, and full employment added to his dream.

If there were obstacles, they were quickly dismissed as being of a "minor" or of a "temporary" nature. The American Indian, his claim on his traditional lands, and his culture, was considered a minor or a temporary obstacle by the ever-increasing hordes of European immigrants.

It was this disregard of the Indian historic claim to the passive use of the environment that fell under the religious zeal of the white man in the name of "Free Enterprise."

It is this conflict of cultures that the reader is asked to remember as the story unfolds. This conflict has been well documented in books and film. Today there is a wide awakening, especially among young adults, that the assault on our ecology can be prevented or reduced.

But for us, who live in Central Minnesota, the problem is all around us.

I invite the reader to visualize the beauty of Kandiyohi County before any white man had intruded upon its pristine beauty. No roads, rails, or power lines across the open waving prairies. Game was plentiful and fish were in abundance in unpolluted lakes. There were no towns, no signs of impacted lake cottages, only an occasional waft of smoke from the cooking fire of a passing Indian hunting party.

It will take the combined effort of all to preserve our heritage and roll back the assault on the natural beauty of our Kandiyohi County Lakes.

J. Gordon Bergquist

COMMENTARY

The State of Minnesota was once covered by giant mountains of ice thousands of years ago. These glaciers retreated north as they melted, leaving us our river systems and our many lakes. They also left us the varieties of soils from black loam to clay, fine sands, and coarse gravels. Only the

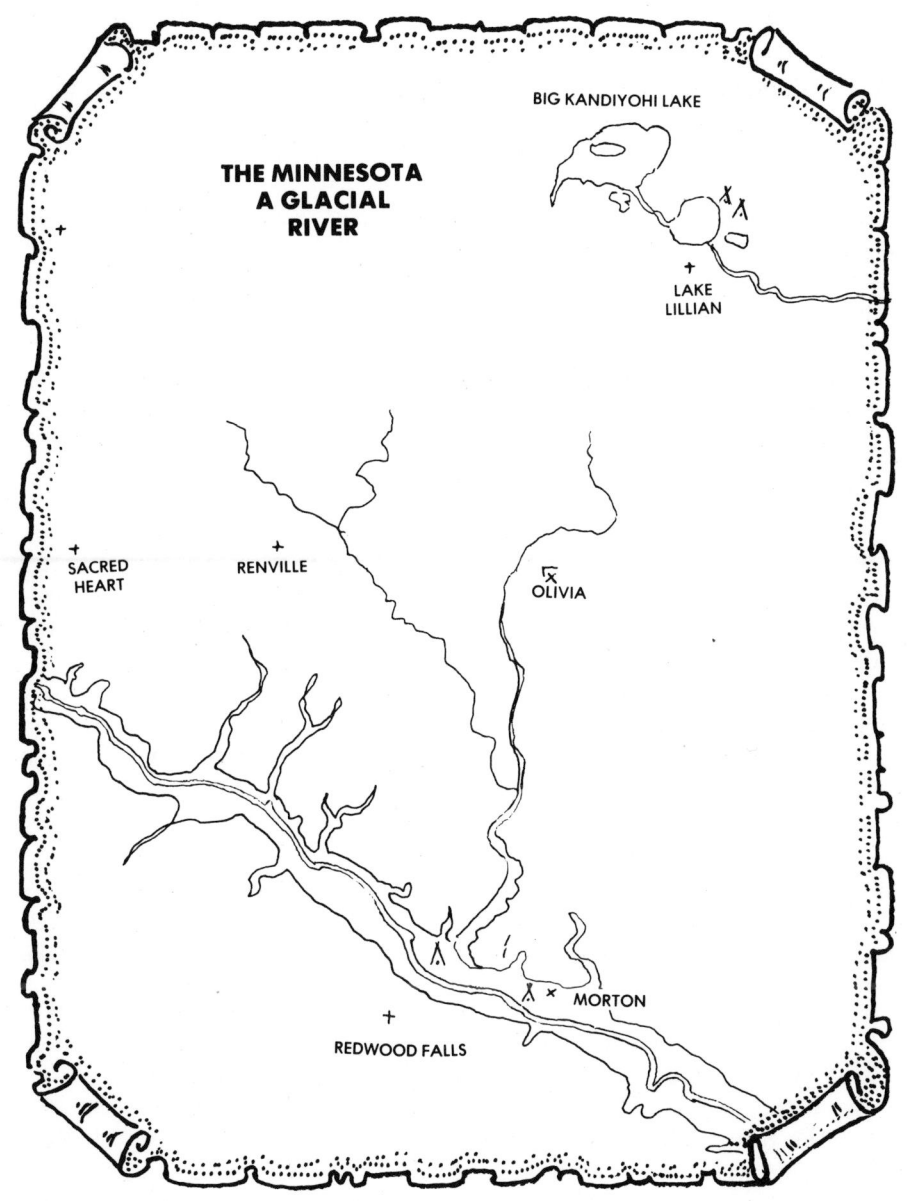

underlying Cambrian Shield with its ancient granite survived in its original form.

Of these river systems, and pertinent to this story, is the Minnesota River which has its source at Browns Valley on the western border of the State, and which flows south and east. Browns Valley is also the source of the Red River which flows north to form the Minnesota-Dakota borders, then into Canada and eventually into the Hudson Bay. The granite outcropping at Browns Valley is the divide determining the directional flow of the two rivers.

The Minnesota flows between high bluffs from its source until it joins the Mississippi near Fort Snelling in South Minneapolis. These high bluffs form a valley which is from one to two miles wide. The stream today is but a hundred feet wide except during the spring runoff when it may be two hundred feet wide. It challenges the imagination to visualize the size of the melting glacial ice cap and the volume of water released with a force that could carve such a broad valley.

The high flat plains on either side were drained each spring by streams that rushed down the bluffs, cutting deep ravines with nearly vertical sides. The ravines attracted a wide variety of trees and shrubs which gave shelter from the wind and trapped the warmth of the sun's rays. This valley was one of the homes of the Sioux, an important key to their survival amidst the wind-swept prairies of Central Minnesota.

The river, said the Sioux, had two natures:

One was a lazy, gently flowing stream a stone's throw wide. This was its character for eleven months. It served as the river highway to all the Sioux encampments at Morton, Redwood Falls, Granite Falls, Montevideo, Lac Qui Parle and Ortonville. It provided water for man and animals. It provided water for bathing and washing and cooking. For young people it was the place to swim, dive and fish in its clear, cold waters.

The other was in spring when it could be an angry giant. A quick thaw of ice and snow on the high prairies could send waters plunging down on a river still frozen over. When this happened, the sudden runoff would add to the total mass that was seeking its way downstream. Ice dams would form lakes which spread over wide sections of the river floor. Groves of trees would also catch the ice and for a short time act as partial dams. All the time the situation would become more dangerous. If a small dam would break loose upriver, its water rushing faster than a man could run, and hurl itself towards another dam downriver, the torrent would tear up everything in its course. The entire character of the river bottom could be altered, leaving only the age-old granite outcroppings. The dammed up muddy lakes lasted just long enough for the silt to settle on what became the bottom land, the richest of soils. Thus, such floods could be beneficial as well as disasterous.

The Sioux tribes who lived along its banks knew and respected the river. The valley was their home, their security, their birthright. And if the river and its valley were precious to them, they could never forget or relinquish the many, jewel-like lakes to the north, the favorite among them Medayto (Green Lake) queen of all the Kandiyohi Lakes.

Because of her size, she was seldom completely calm. But on those rare days it was easy to understand why she was the reigning queen of the Kandiyohi Lakes. Many lakes had sandy beaches, but Medayto had sandy beaches on all sides. She was blessed with a gravel bottom which restricted the growth of vegetation, making the water clear with a touch of emerald green in certain light. Swimmers at eight feet below the surface could see and attract small fish close enough to touch.

It was as if the elements waited in competition to cast their spell. Each could produce in the queen a different mood. When the lake was calm, all nature seemed at rest. The trees were still. The warm sun was to be enjoyed. Her human inhabitants entered into this mood by savoring those lazy days.

On a bright fall day the lake sparkled against a deeper blue sky. There was merriment in her energy. Crisp air was conducive to activity, and its coolness implied cold weather would follow. The wind attacked the trees some days, but they refused to offer up their leaves. As the days passed, the leaves turned color and surrendered, leaving the beautiful wooded shore nothing but bare limbs that would stand half the year before being awakened by spring warmth.

As autumn waned, the wind drove the huge waves against the shore in measured rhythm, enough to swamp a canoe. The waves competed with one another to reach even farther across the fine sand. The repetitious waves, the submissive trees, and the wind in one's ears had the effect of closing in the world to the immediate scene. It brought a mood that was limited and peculiar to Green Lake.

In winter she traded her emerald waves for sheets of glaring, glossy ice. A man could walk on two inches of clear ice and have the sensation of walking on water as he peered into her emerald depths. As she froze and expanded, huge sections challenged each other for dominance, irresistable forces locked in a test of will. Ice floes, miles in length, reared up in opposing force like rams in combat. Their booming traveled like lightning and sounded like thunder. The entire mass was often jolted upward more than two feet. Sometimes the opposing forces were depressed downward in their conflict. This allowed water from below to flood the depressed floes. When weighted down and insulated by deep snow, this water could become treacherous. The expansion force exerted itself against the shores in every direction. The shores of sand gave in, allowing the ice mass to slide inward, and with the aid of winds, upward like great frozen breakers. Nothing could withstand its force. Trees, banks, rocks, all were pushed ahead of the expansion. Under a baleful moon and clear sky, the below-zero temperatures produced ice crystals in the air to create sun dogs flanking the sun during the short, but brilliant winter days.

The Sioux would have preferred to live the year around in the Kandiyohi Lakes region, especially around Green Lake. There was an abundance of game and fish as well as a wide variety of herbs and berries. However, under pressure of battles lost to the Chippewas, it was sometimes necessary for them to retreat to the Minnesota River bottom lands sixty miles across the prairies to the south. Although they missed the lakes, these vast grasslands provided buffalo, deer and elk. The bottom lands were an excellent place to spend the winter, but the distance across the prairie made them feel exiled. The yearning to return was a natural feeling, a matter of pride.

The Chippewas of long ago lived to the east in the Great Lakes area. Pressure from the great Iroquois Nation had forced them to seek lands frequented by the Sioux in Michigan and Wisconsin. But the Sioux were widely scattered. The Chippewas coming by flotillas of canoes, were able to drive first one group, then another, to give up their territories. This pressure took the rivalry into Minnesota. Here the many lakes with much food and game became a great prize. In the end the Chippewas held the deep, clear northern lakes surrounded by virgin pines. The Sioux claimed the more shallow, southerly lakes which were scattered across the Minnesota prairies. The Kandiyohi Lakes, with Green Lake (Medayto) as its center, were the focus of many battles in the distant past, with each side remembering its periods of conquest.

The Chippewas living as far as three hundred miles north had good reasons to move south to meet the spring thaw. The streams ran with fish much earlier. There were more small, warm ponds. These offered an abundance of beaver, muskrat, fox and mink. Later there were duck eggs, berries, roots and herbs not found in their northern home. It was an easy journey for people adept at building and paddling canoes. The Mississippi brought them south. The Crow Rivers brought them west into the Kandiyohi Lakes. They enjoyed the beauty of the Kandiyohi Lakes with their variety of deciduous trees. The early fishing trips were gradually extended until summer encampments were made.

Their numbers at Green Lake constantly increased. Soon the main camp at the inlet by Old Mill Inn (Lower Falls) numbered over a hundred wigwams. Near the outlet there were another hundred. A group of twenty-five were at the southwest shore at present-day Spicer, and at Nest Lake were fifty. Koronis and Diamond Lakes had approximately fifty. Usually there was a group in the New London area, and others moved around the area in groups of ten or more. In all, there were about a thousand inhabitants, including children.

Whichever tribe occupied the Kandiyohi Lakes, invariably they chose the areas surrounding the falls where the Karishon emptied into Green Lake (Old Mill site) because it allowed travel in many directions. Using the Crow River, one could go north to New London, or one could go south towards Willmar by a series of portages. It was also possible to go to Diamond Lake and also east through Lake Calhoun, then east ninety miles to the Mississippi by way of the Middle Fork of the Crow River.

This camp had features that had always attracted men. It was a beautiful setting. The stream, fed from beds of glacial sands farther to the north, offered clean, clear water throughout the year. The high wooded knolls, now known as the Rice Estate was an ideal place for wigwams. This sheltered north shore enjoyed the south winds as they cooled in crossing the huge lake. In cold days the heavily wooded knolls were a perfect windbreak.

Here, on Green Lake, the Chippewas had established their summer sovereignty before the white man's advent. The Sioux, defeated, driven south, humiliated, wanted revenge. In their scattered homes, but mainly in the Minnesota River Valley, they planned that someday they would defeat the enemy in decisive battle.

Someday, the Kandiyohi Lakes, burial place of their ancestors, would be theirs again, forever.

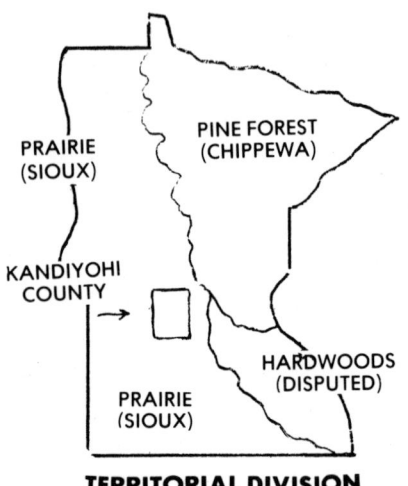

TERRITORIAL DIVISION

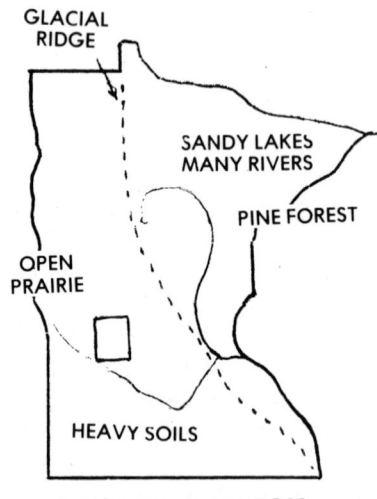

LAND COMPARISON

COMPARATIVE FOOD SUPPLY

TRANSPORTATION AND HOUSING

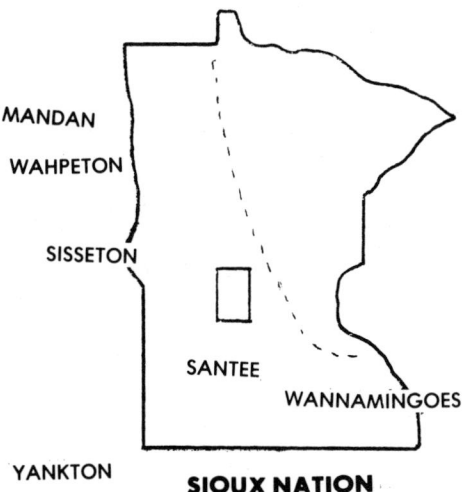
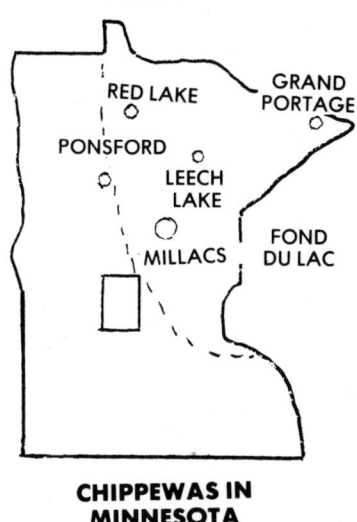

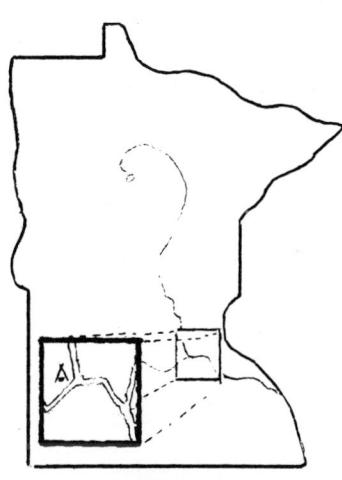

PRINCIPAL CHARACTERS

Minnetaka..................... principal character
Tya.................... Minnetaka's grandmother
Kitsey (White Swan)....................... heroine
Kiyi................... Minnetaka's closest friend

OTHER CHARACTERS

Weasel...................... Minnetaka's friend
Yellow Bee................... Minnetaka's friend
Red Sun, deer hunt leader..... Tya's younger brother
Blue Feather................. deer hunter captured
High Hawk.................. deer hunter captured
White Wolf........... Minnetaka's father (deceased)
Grey Dove.......... Minnetaka's mother (deceased)
Red Bird................ Kitsey's Chippewa mother
Hokey....................... Kitsey's stepfather
Grey Dog................... Chief of Santee Sioux
Long Walk.................. Chief of Sisseton Tribe
Bear Tooth.......................... Chief Sioux
Iron Hand.................... Chief of Chippewas
Cass Teo..................... Chippewa renegade
Ghost Raven...................... Sioux trapper
One Finger Left Behind............ Chippewa scout
Jotee................... wrestler at Granite Festival

Locations renamed to sound more Indian:

Green Lake........................... Medayto
Spicer Area...................... Medayto Prairie
Lake Lillian.............................. Mayto
Kandiyohi Lakes...... All lakes in Kandiyohi County
Morton Redwood Falls Area........... Santee Camp
New London Lakes...... Monongalia Chain of Lakes
New London Dam..... Upper Falls of Karishon River
Middle Fork of Crow River...... The Karishon River
Old Mill Inn Dam Site. Lower Falls of Karishon River,
                also called Medayto Falls
Four Lakes....... Norway Lake, West Norway Lake,
            Games Lake, and Middle Lake
Lake Andrew..................... Moose Call Lake
Mount Tom...................... Moose Call Hill
George and Henderson................. High Lakes
Calhoun Lake......................... Loon Lake
Diamond Lake...................... Lake Manah
Foote and Willmar Lakes............. Teepee Lakes
Sperry House Hill.. Teepee Knoll (Willmar Townsite)
Hanover........................... Portage Falls
Robbins Island...................... Victor Island
St. Anthony Falls..................... The Big Falls
Fort Snelling Promontory......... The Great Bluff or
                    The High Meadow

1 The Gathering
2 Lake Lillian - Mayto
3 Deer Hunt
4 The Enemy
5 Return To Valley
6 The Festival
7 Tya Remembers
8 The Buffalo Hunt
9 Kitsey Captured
10 Council of War
11 A Scouting Mission
12 Kitsey in Captivity
13 Enemy Territory
14 The Meeting
15 Ecstacy and Pain
16 War Council
17 Negotiation
18 The Battle
19 Chippewa Deception
20 Cass-Teo
21 The Rescue
22 The Mississippi
23 The Wedding Celebration
24 The Homecoming

Gathering of Tribes

1
The Gathering

Fingers of dust moved into the valley of the Minnesota River below as one tribe after another spurred its ponies toward the large encampment on the valley floor. Minnetaka, in war paint, sat on his black stallion looking down. He had just turned sixteen.

The Wanamingoes and the Winnebagoes were coming from down river to the east. The Ogalalas and the Poncas had already arrived from the Niobrara River in Nebraska. The Wahpetons and the Sissetons were coming from the west. The Santees, his tribe, and the Wanamingoes were from this valley. These were of the great Sioux Nation who called themselves Dakotahs.

This concentration had been many moons in arranging. Their mission was simple, but dangerous: They were here to settle for all time the dominance of the Central Minnesota lakes, particularly the cluster called the Kandiyohi Group. The Chippewas, also known as the Ojibways, were gradually expanding southward into the Kandiyohi area from their main camps at Mille Lacs Lake and Leech Lake. Their summer wigwams dotted the shore of the huge emerald water called Medayto. Clashes between hunting and war parties had been often and bloody. Now it was rumored that the Chippewas were building permanent winter shelters. This could not go unchallenged. The honor of the entire Sioux Nation was at stake, hence the many pow-wows and now final agreement: the Chippewas must go, and forevermore be banished from the Kandiyohi Lakes.

Minnetaka had fond memories of those lakes. His mind went back to those long summer days he had spent with his grandmother Tya at beautiful Mayto. He had been thirteen years old then. It seemed like yesterday, the details still fresh, as he recalled the images of childhood, and pondered the end of his carefree boyhood.

2
Lake Lillian - Mayto

She moved slowly against a backdrop of old oaks with the same protective coloration of a hen mallard on her nest. She was a creature of and a part of this sunlit wooded park that formed the northeast shore of gleaming Lake Mayto. Slowly she spread the hot coals to evenly heat the rack of drying fish, adding a few sticks at a time to hold the fire to her patient time table.

Her face had the strong, bony features that marked her a Santee Sioux. The deep wrinkles combined to suggest conviction, wisdom, patience. The net of tiny wrinkles told of age, suffering and resignation. She was called Tya, "The One with the Long Memory." Her gnarled hands revealed three short fingers, each an offering for the loss of a warrior husband and two sons, each a page in her history.

This was the Moon of the Black Grapes, the last days of summer. This was the final journey for winter food. The plums, walnuts, butternuts and hazel nuts were ripening. Gooseberries and cranberries were at their peak. As each fruit ripened, the birds and creatures of the forest also awaited the harvest. One must be ready. Tya could remember the seasons good and bad. It was she who set the times the younger women of the camp should plan their journey for winter food. It was she who evaluated each individual's efforts by offering a few grunts of approval as her personal award of merit.

Already the blue of the sky was deepening. Green vegetation was taking on touches of tan. The days were warm, even hot, but evening brought cooler air. Fall was approaching. It was a busy time of preparation. Careful preparation must be made for enough food as well as warm shelter. A prolonged winter with heavy snow and below zero temperatures could mean starvation and disease in the camp. Most adults had had personal experience with these disasters. Winters were remembered by their severity.

Tya's mind was as occupied as her hands; now it dwelled momentarily on shelter and the necessary preparations.

The Sioux teepees were erected by tying the ends of three long poles together near the top. More poles were then leaned against this crotch. Birch bark or skins covered the outside. An opening at the top allowed smoke to escape. The fire was in the center. Space was allocated, acknowledging respect. Adults were always seated nearest the door. Daughters were next to their mothers. Personal belongings were kept wrapped in skins and kept under the beds. Beds were along the outside perimeters of the teepees and were used as seats during the day. In winter, additional skins were also hung on the inside of the teepees. Additional warmth was possible by piling cedar boughs and grass and snow on the outside walls of the teepee. Food storage was in log shelters nearby, and in pits covered with fine moss and soft hay.

Tya sat down heavily on a log facing the harsh sun as it lit the millions of moving diamonds on the rippled lake. It was like her to fret over winter preparations, proper shelter, plenty of stored food. Her small eyes narrowed as she peered through the film of blue smoke that hung in the sheltered woods. She sought out the half dozen naked boys at play some distance down the sandy beach. She had no way of picking out her grandson. It was enough that she knew that they were busy as a group. She knew without really seeing them that their bobbing heads and bare bottoms would alternate as they dove for clams in the pure water. It brought to her mind a family of pelicans as they discover a school of shiner minnows.

The clams would flavor her soup. Her recipe this time would contain the white, tender hearts of cattails. This was a delicacy featured on these seasonal pilgrimages.

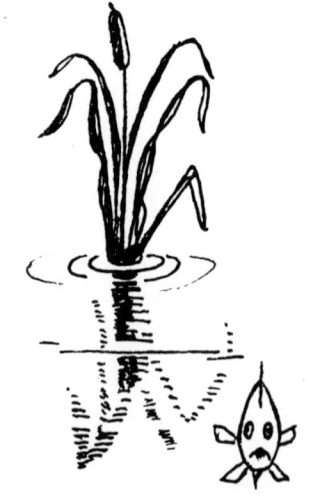

These pilgrimages were an annual journey to gather food. Because Tya had spent so many summers of her youth in the Kandiyohi Lake country, she was, by silent choice, the leader. Her Santee Sioux tribe had been driven out of the lake country by the Chippewa. Their latest excursion into Sioux territory happened just a few years ago. A confrontation was now becoming certain.

Minnetaka watched the activity below from his tree-less promontary. From this high vantage point he could see south across the valley, and north across the prairie and both up and down the river that ran below him. His friend, Kiyi, came up the trail of the steep ravine to join him. As young scouts their mission was to direct incoming tribes to settlement areas. This preparation for war had its beginning in an incident a few summers ago when Minnetaka and his friend Kiyi had their first experience with the enemy, the hated Chippewa.

3
Deer Hunt

It was late afternoon. They were camped at Mayto. As Minnetaka surfaced from a deep dive, Kiyi rapped on his head. Just before dunking him in return, he saw his friend's anguished face. He was pointing far down the shore to the west.

"Look, Minnetaka, horses coming!"

"Tell the others to follow," Minnetaka said, diving toward shore and emerging in shallow water. From there, he ran half-stooped up the sandy bank into the shadow of the hardwoods. Then, veering, he picked up the path that led back to where Tya sat smoking her short pipe and tending the fires.

"Tya — horses coming fast!" he cried, out of breath.

"Where?"

"Along the shore to the west."

"How many?" she asked.

"I can't tell. Maybe six."

"Is one white?"

"No, but one has a white head, Tya."

"Then they are our hunters, but something is wrong. They are returning from the wrong direction. They weren't expected until dusk. Hurry! Get the other boys to help. Put sand on the fire. Collect the food in bundles and move them back into the brush. Leave everything else and go north through the woods into the deep cattail swamp. Leave no easy trail. Quickly now!"

Tya turned to Kiyi and ordered, "Run, warn the women picking berries. Tell them to leave their baskets and come nearer the camp without showing themselves. Stay with them until we call."

After a quick examination of the stripped campsite, Tya moved cautiously towards a clump of trees near the lake bank. In the shadows she was camouflaged. By the slightest movements she could search the shore for the returning hunting party. They would cross a small, dry inlet. She could count them there. Her eyes, black and shiny, revealed that familiar tension which came from knowing danger.

Eight men had gone to hunt deer north of the Lake Wagonga chain of lakes. The Chippewas, thus far, had not ventured far south of Medayto. Therefore, food-gathering in the Mayto area had not been considered a great risk by the Sioux. The hunt had been led by Tya's youngest brother, Red Sun, his two sons, and five other braves. What could be wrong? Her eyes, still fixed on the inlet, at last saw the party appear in full sunlight. Yes, there was her brother with the white-headed stallion, but he was followed by only five. So, two men were missing. The party was moving fast, but evidently not being pursued.

As the hunting party, moving in single file, neared the camp, it was as if they formed a long bobbin that passed slowly through yarns of alternating bright sun and deep shadow. The anticipation mounted as their dust became visible and the muffled hoofbeats became louder and sharper. The hunters entered the campsite in a cloud of dust; their heaving ponies, glistening with sweat, seemed relieved as the riders dismounted. One rider gathered the ropes, and walking stiffly led the ponies behind a plum thicket that grew among the hardwoods.

The hunters, caked with dust, laid aside their bows, arrows and blankets. Out of the brush came the young boys. Moments later the women moved into the circle to hear what had alarmed the hunting party, particularly what had happened to the two missing hunters.

Red Sun, oldest of the group, confirmed the suspicions of all with the single hated word, "Chippewas!" He comforted them by saying there was no immediate danger, but that they must return to the Minnesota River as soon as possible. Whether they liked it or not, the Chippewas were encamped in force but a day's journey to the north, and they were now foraging further and further south.

As the women and children sat in a circle, somber and fearful, Red Sun narrated. Minnetaka never forgot that afternoon.

The Wagonga drive for deer was tradition for the Santee. It was a strategic maneuver that drove the deer out of a long wooded area into a narrow neck where hunters in wait could get open shots at close range. The hunters chosen to drive the deer entered the area from the prairie to the west. On the south was the shore of long, narrow Lake Wagonga. To their left was a swamp. The drivers moved slowly and quietly, preferring to move the deer very slowly rather than having them take flight. The hunters in wait wanted a sure kill because this was food needed for the approaching winter.

This day, Tya's brother Red Sun sent the two best marksmen around the swamp to await the approach of the deer. Then each driver was spaced to prevent the deer from slipping behind the drivers. It took patience. A deer in flight would alarm all others, and thus became a difficult target. An arrow must find the heart or lungs to insure death soon enough for the carcass to be found. It was vital that they bring back at least two deer; four would be cause for celebration.

The hunt had started the day before with the eight men leaving at dawn. They were to be gone two days. The first day was spent in the woods north of Big Kandiyohi Lake. By careful driving, one deer was killed. The night was spent on the east shore of Lake Wagonga. Little Kandiyohi, Kasota, and Minnetaga Lakes stretched to the east.

The following morning, Wagonga was circled by traveling around the west end. From there the drive was east along the north shore. There was little need to hurry. The deer wandered about at night, moving back into wooded areas at dawn. By mid-morning they were bedded down for the day.

This was the time to start the drive. The deer would be reluctant to move very far. Their first instinct was to move aside and allow an intruder to pass. This was why several drivers were necessary. The deer could detect even the most cautious movements of a hunter. The deer would slowly move away, and upon hearing the second hunter would gradually move eastward. Waiting in good cover with open areas in front of them were the stationary hunters.

Often when the wind was right and the leaves underfoot were soft and moist, a hunter could walk within sight of a doe and her fawns as they lay resting. The hunter would remain still lest his presence send them running in headlong flight. By standing motionless, the hunter would wait until the noise of a more distant hunter put the doe on alert and cause her to move slowly away.

The two best bowmen were sent to conceal themselves at the end of the drive. Tying their horses they advanced on foot, crossing areas of open prairie. As the drive progressed, the deer were often sighted, and the anticipation grew. No driver had the right to shoot at a deer that was moving toward the hidden bowmen, but all hoped to have a deer turn and come directly at them. This would happen only at the end of the drive.

As this drive neared its end, Red Sun explained that three deer were seen moving towards the concealed braves. One went down, another was hit but continued on in full flight. He had watched in alarm as one of his disciplined bowmen ran eagerly after the wounded deer. It was unforgiveable for him to leave his stand. Suddenly there was a wild yell from the same hunter. It seemed that he had found the crippled deer and was cheering his own marksmanship. But, there was something strange, something was wrong.

It was no Santee Sioux yell. This was not a cry from a member of his disciplined team of hunters. This was the enemy. They must have been shadowing the hunting party. The bold presence indicated a group of some strength.

All he thought about then was to save his men from capture or death. They must now outflank the enemy to recover their horses and ride to safety. Blue Feather was captured for certain, and there was no sign of High Hawk.

It was time to retreat. Knowing the woods gave them the advantage, but the trap that usually proved so effective in trapping deer could now be working in reverse with the hunters becoming the hunted. An imitation call of the crow was repeated, their rallying signal for danger, and the entire party retreated.

The horses were recovered. Their comrades were either dead or captive, depending on the mood of the Chippewa leader. However, brutal murder was the equivalent of a signal for all-out war. A leader of a small group would hesitate to take that responsibility. It was more likely that the captives would be taken to the main camp at Medayto. There, the Chief's Council would decide their fate. Often torture, humiliation and warnings would be such, that if freed, captives would serve as messengers of hate upon return to their own people. More often, an opposite effect was achieved, and bitterness between the tribes increased.

It was late afternoon when Red Sun decreed that they must leave immediately. They were probably in no immediate danger because the Chippewas were unfamiliar with this Mayto area, and because they probably returned triumphantly with their two Santee captives to camp. The Sioux were outnumbered and at a disadvantage. There was no point in taking risks when they needed the food they had already gathered for the long winter.

4
The Enemy

The small party departed as silently and quickly as possible. The young carried camp equipment. The women carried dried fish, berries and nuts. The horses dragged a travois which consisted of a pair of long poles upon which dressed game was lashed.

Minnetaka's recall of that homeward journey was in sharp detail. Fear, anger, frustration, electrified all members of the party which moved at the same pace as the walking horses. This pace was brisk for adults and almost a half-run for the young boys. Coarse grass, thistles and thorny brambles scratched and cut his near-nude body. Even so, at his early age he sensed an obligation to be a part of the total effort. He was challenged to be serious, mature, a candidate for the distinction of future warrior status. Any outcry or complaint would have been an embarassment to his family.

The caravan moved without stopping until dark. Camp was made in the long grass of the open prairie. The horses were hidden in willow thickets near a stream. Though they might be safe, Red Sun ordered that no fires be lit.

An evening meal of dried fish and pemmican was eaten while prairie beds were prepared. These consisted of coarse grass piled to ankle height. This gave cushion support and insulation from the damp ground. Fine prairie hay was then piled on, its aroma pleasant as a mild breeze moved from the south. Soft buckskin provided a wrap-around covering. It was enough in summer. Constant exposure the year around had conditioned the Sioux to withstand a great deal of prolonged cold. Their simple explanation was: "Sioux strong, Sioux hard, whole body like face."

Lying on his pallet of grass Minnetaka listened to the crickets and frogs. In the nearby swamp he heard "boompa-boompa," the call of the bittern. Above him the Great Spirit had lit a million stars. In silence he meditated:

He lives up there, He sees me, He knows I am here. With the Earth Mother He provides for all of us, His children.

A star streaked across the sky. What did it mean? Who could tell him what it meant? Was it perhaps a signal from his brave, dead father?

As the Santee party slept, the Chippewa war party was still celebrating its minor victory. To remind the retreating enemy they had out-witted the day before, they decided to send a visible challenge.

This dark night they chose a tall, dead cottonwood that stood on a knoll overlooking Lake Wagonga. The young braves gathered tall, dry grass and tied it into huge bundles. One brave climbed to the top of the tree, and with his buckskin rope hoisted the bundles to the top. When all was ready, a pole with fire at one end was passed up. The tree became a monstrous torch against a dark sky. It was as symbolic as a clenched fist.

The solitary Santee guard saw the light far away on the northern horizon and felt its implication. Yes, this day belonged to the Chippewa, but there would be other days.

5
Return To Valley

As the returning hunting party reached the river bluffs, the dry yellow and tan prairie grass was behind them. The valley before them was of deeper shades of green. These were their pastured bottom lands. Horses roamed the area by day while deer and elk ventured out of their brushy hiding during the night. The slopes of the upper bluffs showed bare yellow clay washouts. Interspersed were clumps of tall broom grass. Where nothing else could grow, the common cedars survived. In some mysterious way they grew separate from each other, their deep green contrasting with the short-yellow-green grass. Large patches of inpenetrable plum thickets grew on the gentle slopes, sharing space with groves of red sumac whose broad leaves made a huge shade umbrella pierced with shafts of sunlight.

When their permanent camp at Red Wood came into view, they were relieved and overjoyed. They saw the smoke from many cooking fires rising in towers until it reached the altitude of the surrounding bluffs. From there gentle breezes carried it southward in horizontal wisps that soon disappeared.

They were greeted by children running to meet them, hoping for a sample of berries, nuts and, if lucky, some honey. Older boys were curious about the game that was brought back. They were hoping for the pelt of a bear, a wolf or a wild cat. The women gathered to unpack the horses and begin cutting up game and distributing some to each family. Skins had to be stretched and scraped before tanning. Old Tya, weary from the journey, retired to her teepee.

The six braves were silent as they turned over their horses to young boys for tethering in the grass meadows. Then Red Sun went directly to see Chief Grey Dog. After a few moments he returned to the waiting group and announced that there would be a pow-wow that evening. There were im-

portant issues to discuss.

As darkness fell, all the braves of the Red Wood Camp gathered around a fire in front of Grey Dog's teepee. Minnetaka and Kiyi sat behind the circle in the shadows with other boys their age.

The old chief listened as all the young braves tried to talk at once. Some wanted to form a war party immediately and attack the Chippewa's main camp at Medayto, even though they had no idea of its size. Others demanded a nighttime raid to rescue the two captive warriors.

Grey Dog held up a hand for silence, then spoke: "Soon the Chippewa will leave the Kandiyohi Lakes for their northern homes. Any action must wait until after the long snows. Whatever we plan with our Sioux brothers must be decisive. Yes, the enemy must be driven out, never to return. Anything less will not be worth the bloodshed.

"This is not a time for rage and foolhardy battle against a stronger force. I, too, am sad and angry that Blue Feather and High Hawk have been lost to us.

"The problem is clear, it is serious. It must be dealt with. But ... we must remember that for many, many moons we have fought the Chippewa ... and we have lost more often than we have won."

He sighed heavily, his lined face ruddy in the fireglow, as if too weary to find the right words. Nobody stirred, nobody whispered. They respected his wisdom.

"Victory ..." he went on, " ... victory is the result of careful planning more than of individual courage. We must meet often with our Sioux brothers until we have a master war plan and are certain that we have the strength to defeat the enemy and teach it respect. I am convinced it is the only way."

Minnetaka listened intently to the war of words which followed. The older braves tried to bring about unanimous agreement, siding with Grey Dog, but the younger ones were still keenly disappointed and humiliated, arguing that this was not the way of the proud Sioux of days gone by.

Finally, as the fire died down to embers, the mature, calmer faction persevered and a pipe was passed from one to another to seal the agreement. Battle with the Chippewa would wait until after the season of the long snows.

Minnetaka, erect and alert on his black stallion, remembering the wisdom of Grey Dog, looked down into the valley with pride as the many Sioux tribes gathered.

Minnetaka spoke to Kiyi, "It has been worth the waiting, even if the planning has taken three seasons of long snows. The Chippewa will be defeated."

6
The Festival

The annual harvest festival was held during the Moon of Falling Leaves at the Granite Falls in the beautiful Minnesota River Valley with its back waters, granite islands and out-croppings. The central location made it less than two day's travel by canoe for most Minnesota tribes. Each tribe set up camp for a four-day festival. The time would be taken up with feasting, singing, dancing and games and contests of all kinds for young and old. Young folks of each tribe intermingled, and through this annual gathering were able to take note of one another.

Minnetaka had seen the girl many times without really noticing her. She lived here at the Granite Falls. Most likely his vague recollections of her were from harvest festivals of years past. There were many children, and the boys and girls looked alike as they swam. Out of these many running, splashing, yelling young people her face would emerge.

Perhaps it was the time all were diving for river clams that he truly saw her. His brown body was more down than up, collecting clams and tossing them on the rock ledge. The other boys were acquaintances from other tribes. The same groups were often together.

The water at the Granite Falls was always the clearest anywhere. Standing above it one could see huge broken sections of granite on its bottom. Between the sections a fine grey sand could be found. It was his search along these sand deposits that brought him face to face with another swimmer. Spying the same clam at the same time their hands met. With a determined twist he tore the clam from the other boy's grasp. It was play, but competitive play. But who was the boy? They surfaced together. It was not a boy!

As their heads broke the surface they looked at each other, mouths open, hair clinging. She laughed, partly because he was too surprised to react. In a quick movement she half-cupped her palm, and shooting it forward sent a spray of water towards his open mouth. She left him gagging. Then, diving under the water like an otter, she swam upstream towards other swimmers. It was the briefest of encounters.

Could a girl be a friend? Yes, she could be his friend. A friend who could swim like a boy, a friend who could laugh and tease like a boy. But she was pretty, too, not at all like a boy. He did not even know her name.

Since there were hundreds of adults and children in constant motion during the activities, Minnetaka found himself scanning the crowd on the unlikely chance that he might see her again. He saw her finally, but she was busy laughing with other girls. She did not notice him. He watched her from a distance. Yes, she was pretty; even when she was not smiling her face was pleasant.

During the days that followed Minnetaka competed in the distance races and the foot races up to the top of the river bluffs. He led a team of four in a relay race that involved running, climbing, jumping and swimming. There were no prizes, just approval and vocal support.

His main interests were the games of skill and strength. He was a leader among the half dozen boys of his age from the Redwood Santee tribe. Here, however, the rivalry was with boys from the other encampments. His tall, lean frame was deceiving. Daily running, jumping, and wrestling made him both strong and quick. Tya had said that from his father he had inherited a sense of timing and balance which made his movements seem effortless. He wrestled for fun and often showed a slight smile. Win or lose he was a friendly competitor. But his winning brought out envy and sometimes rage in some of his competitors, many of whom were heavier, older and from larger settlements. Each had his cheering section. Defeat was not always easy to accept from this tall, wiry lad from the Red Wood Camp.

This year he would be remembered for his bout with Jotee, the pride of the Sissetons. Being younger, he had been defeated by Jotee other years. But he had grown fast. Now it would be a closer match.

After losing two quick falls, Jotee became enraged. He charged Minnetaka and succeeded in forcing his head to the ground. With this advantage he dropped his full weight onto Minnetaka's back, an obvious foul. Minnetaka groaned, unable to rise. There were many growls of disapproval. Jotee ignored the protests and snarled, "Do you want more?" Minnetaka rose slowly and quietly answered, "Yes."

Now there was no smile on his wide boyish face. His distended nostrils reminded all that he was a runner. His eyes deep set and shiny would time the attack. The onlookers held their breath. Jotee was confused. He saw Minnetaka's left foot move - then it happened.

Dropping low in a cat-like movement Minnetaka caught Jotee around the waist, and forced him through the circle of spectators towards the river. They ended up on a flat rock ledge above the water, Jotee struggling but helpless in Minnetaka's grip. At the edge he released Jotee, allowing him to stand. He then stepped back and at the same time tapped Jotee's chest just enough to unbalance him. Waving his arms frantically, Jotee plunged backward into the river.

Everybody laughed and would repeat the story. With each repetition Minnetaka's reputation would grow. He would become marked as a young man who would more easily lead than follow.

The last day arrived with much ceremony. It had been a good year except for the humiliation at Lake Wagonga. The gods must be thanked for their blessings. Also, one must petition the gods for a good winter free from starvation and disease. The drums beat continuously to the loud chants, sometimes in solo, sometimes all in unison invoking the blessings of the gods. This was accompanied by dancers in brightly colored costumes, some comic, some in hideous war paint.

Minnetaka was fascinated by the stacatto of the drums. It stirred his blood, and he could feel the rhythmic response of the dancers to its insistent beat. There was that call to come and join, to be a part of this group who were declaring their oneness, their unanimity. They were one in spiritual faith. They were one in a pledge of death before disgraceful conduct in battle. They were also one people with one history behind them and a future ahead of them only if they pledged their collective allegiance to one another. The drum beat and the plaintive singing was to dwell in his mind for weeks. Next year he might be ready to express his faith. Next year, he, too, might be able to dance to the call of the drums.

Although the tribal council of the eight Sioux tribes had been in session several times during the festival, they still could not agree unanimously on exactly when would be the best time to drive the Chippewas out of the Kandiyohi Lakes. Minnetaka learned only the general facts of these sessions from Red Sun, and as the festival neared its end, it was certain there would be no all-out war before another winter season had passed.

One tribe claimed they needed more horses, another had suffered losses. Others felt that their younger warriors were not battle-ready. And, two leading medicine men stated that the portents were all wrong. So the chiefs agreed to wait, and during the forthcoming moons to exchange ideas and strategies until they could be certain of victory.

After mid-day Tya was already loading the canoe. The trip to their home at Red Wood would take until nightfall. Minnetaka loaded the heavy items for her, but his mind was elsewhere. Would he see the girl again? Would she remember him? After all, the river had been full of swimmers, and she might never remember that encounter or his glimpse of her in the crowd.

The beautiful valley that had been so full of colorful teepees, canoes and costumes was now being emptied as everyone departed. Bands that came by land wound their way single file up the steep bluffs towards the open prairie.

Tya talked to herself as she worked. She explained quietly to each item where it should be placed in the canoe and why. When finished she straightened up to survey the total effect. As she did so she raised her voice in approval. It was this louder voice that told Minnetaka that all was ready to depart.

While Minnetaka went to say a quick goodbye to acquaintences, he saw several girls passing. Yes, it was she again. She was talking and laughing with her friends, never letting her eyes look directly at him.

He found himself playing the same game. His mind was on her, but his voice was trying to answer his friends. He heard himself say, "Yes, we'll wrestle again next year," while in his mind all he wanted to know was her name.

Tya was pushing the canoe away from the rock ledge. It was time to go. The girls meanwhile had walked further downstream. They were out of sight except for the smallest of the group. As she passed near the boys, Minnetaka stepped out blocking her path. "Who is the tallest of your friends?" She darted past him, but over shoulder she said, "You must mean White Swan. We call her Kitsey."

With a quick farewell to his friends, Minnetaka leaped into the canoe with the scolding Tya, and they drifted out towards the main current. As the canoe moved downstream it passed the girls standing on a rocky point. All waved, but in silence. Tya in the stern watched as Minnetaka waved in return. The girls had stopped waving when Minnetaka called her name: "Kitsey!" she alone waved. Tya cut sharply to avoid a hidden rock and grumbled. Minnetaka dug into the water vigorously, elated, and the canoe shot out into the stream. They were a good team. Tya steered the course; he provided the power. The even flow of the current gave them time to enjoy the beautiful colors of the fall season in the Minnesota Valley.

As he paddled, he knew that now he would never forget her. It was strange, he thought, how young children of both sexes played together in the innocence of childhood. It was hard to distinguish boys from girls. Rivalry was unknown. But in a few years, sometimes suddenly, it made a difference to the young boys. He supposed that girls noticed the difference, too, but in their own way.

Now any attempt by a girl to participate in boys' sports was met with hostility. The boys were beginning to emulate their fathers and brothers. Play became contest. Running, jumping, swimming, wrestling, hunting had to have winners and losers. Soon the adults became prejudiced spectators and the competition increased. The loser this year would return next year, older, taller and stronger. Girls of this age now had to learn the skills of women. Being attractive in subtle ways was one of those skills.

7
Tya Remembers

As they paddled homeward, he thought how special these late summer days were to both of them. It gave them hours together, which would be less and less as he grew toward manhood. How often she had taught him the way of the Sioux, loving and understanding him, being both father and mother. As he grew she had taught him about the Great Spirit and about the many special gods which inhabited the earth, how he must seek out the good omens for his success and safety.

Sitting before the campfire, suddenly Minnetaka asked, "Tya, tell me, who was my father? Who was my mother?". He had asked when he was nine or ten, feeling he deserved a full explanation. He had asked other times, and she had avoided the subject, and none of the tribe would tell him anything in detail.

"I will tell you. For now, bring water from the spring and move the tethered horses to new grass."

When the tasks were done, and they had eaten a simple meal, she stoked the fire and told him to sit down. Her face in the firelight was sad and intense.

"Now I will tell you." She clasped her hands tightly. "Your father was my first-born son. Your grandfather, my husband Red Fox, was a chief of the small Wanamingo tribe. We lived downstream near Mankato. During an epidemic of lung fever your grandfather died and the remainder of the tribe moved to Red Wood. At the time your father, "White Wolf, was seventeen and without a wife.

"There were disadvantages to our joining the Santee Sioux. I was Sioux, but a Wanamingo was considered something less by the Santees. White Wolf found himself an outsider in spite of his obvious fitness for warrior status. In contests of skill his winning was cause for envy among many in the tribe, both young and old. It was about this time that he became an interested suitor competing for the attention of Grey Dove who would become your mother. Because she was a daughter of a lesser chief this was not welcomed by her parents.

"Grey Dove had other suitors. One after another were ignored by her. Without something to offer her family it was quite out of the question for White Wolf to expect any consideration. Grey Dove, wanting to please her parents, had not indicated she had a preference. It was not her right. Her father would make that decision when he was satisfied with the dowry offered in exchange for her.

"In early spring our tribe was visited by a traveling horse trader from the Ponca Tribe to the southwest on the Missouri River. Because horses were new on our prairies, he was in much demand. A horse gave a mounted warrior such an advantage that it was worth anything one tribe could offer in exchange. Literally, it meant the survival of the band.

"He was old, wise and crafty, that horse trader. He noticed Grey Dove, then sixteen years of age. It was easy to read his mind. He would trade three horses for her hand. One was a large, strong black stallion, the others smaller mares. Now the band would have horses, and in time the mares would produce colts. The Chief was enthusiastic. Grey Dove's father would have the stallion. It seemed an ideal move for the safety of the entire tribe. For all except Grey Dove and White Wolf.

"An agreement was made. The trader was going downstream to the confluence of the Minnesota and the Mississippi Rivers where he would sell his last six horses in trade for copper arrowheads and knives from the Great Lakes. This would take two weeks. He would then return for his bride-to-be."

Tya had paused for a few moments, her forehead furrowed in deep thought, to poke in the fire. Even then, Minnetaka remembered, he had realized how painful it was for her to tell the story. But she sighed deeply and went on.

"Your father made a decision. If horses were so vital, then he would get horses of his own. He knew the tribes many days travel to the south had horses. He knew also that horses were so often stolen that a present owner seldom had a real legitimate claim to his horses. He would travel alone and steal a dowry for Grey Dove. In his desperation he knew he must confide in her, for she was the reason for his plan.

"He saw her coming from the river. She was alone. He went to meet her, knowing many would be watching. There was no time for formalities. He asked her to be his wife. He understood her father's plans for her marriage, but he, too, expected to have horses. He proposed that if he did not return in ten days he would not return at all. If he returned with the horses he wanted her to speak firmly to her father in his behalf because he loved her and wanted her to be his woman forever. She replied that it seemed impossible, but that she would speak for him, and wished him a safe journey.

"He loaded food in a parafleche and departed without notice to anyone except me. He planned to walk eight hours, then sleep four hours and walk another six. The fourth day would put him at the Missouri, home of the Kiowas. The Kiowas were crafty traders and thieves. It would be their horses he would steal.

"The location of the Kiowa camp took an extra day. The rising smoke of their fires gave him their location, but he was disappointed when he discovered they were across the Missouri River. This river was five times as wide as the Minnesota, but was at low summer level. The bottom was a series of sand bars and pools. It was hard to know which was the moving main stream. Like the Minnesota, it was filled with dead trees and roots as aftermath of the spring runoffs.

"A brisk northwest wind was blowing. White Wolf decided he must swim the river, then light a prairie fire upwind. A narrow fire moving rapidly to the left of the camp would cause great smoke and great concern in the camp. It was a gamble that the smoke would cut off the horses from the Kiowas' view.

"The horses were tethered close to the camp. He chose the ones he wanted in advance as he hid below the river bank, a stallion, a mare and a colt stallion. By pulling up the tether ropes and leading the horses below the river embankment, he would be out of sight in a matter of minutes. The greater problem was to keep control of the half-wild animals as he led and drove them across the treacherous river bed.

"Hidden by the embankment he moved upstream until the camp was downwind. He then lashed together four huge, dry tumbleweeds to make a ball high as his head. To this he added soft, dry grass by weaving it into the center of the ball. When all was ready he struck his flint and rock of iron. The sparks ignited the pulverized moss and in a moment the ball of weeds was aflame. As it burned it created its own updraft making it lighter. The wind then lifted it and it tumbled downwind spreading fire as it rolled."

Tya had chuckled, her black eyes glittering.

"The Kiowa camp came alive with much screaming and dogs barking. Women, children and a few men went out to divert the fire from the camp. A mass of white smoke rolled along the ground. The plan worked perfectly. During the confusion White Wolf raced for the three chosen horses. The fire had excited them and they were hard to handle. The stallion sounded a shrill call, but soon all had been led below the embankment.

Kiowa Horses

"All went well until the main stream was reached. Here White Wolf went behind the horses, whipping them with the tether ropes until they began to swim. Once started it was all he could do to hold the ropes as he was dragged through the water by the separated horses.

"Upon crossing the current he raced ahead of the horses, leading them out of the river bed. Reaching a brushy draw he paused for breath. Looking back he saw the Kiowas still fighting the fire. No one had seen his daring daylight raid.

"He looked carefully at the horses he had stolen. The stallion was spotted white and brown. The large mare was brown. The young stallion was almost white. He had chosen well. Since the mare seemed gentle, he talked to her, rubbed her ears and breathed very softly into her nostrils. It was an old trick he had heard told. It had a calming effect, and she let him mount. They moved swiftly toward Sioux country. In one day they would be in friendly territory among the Sissetons.

"After nine days of strenuous travel your father was back with his three horses. The excitement spread through camp. It was a victory for all. The horses were an advantage in travel, in battle and in hunting buffalo. White Wolf was a hero. But the question still remained. Did he qualify as a suitor for Grey Dove? And the horse trader, did he come back? Yes, but all the tribe was in favor of Grey Dove marrying White Wolf.

"As evening fell, White Wolf went to the teepee of Grey Dove's father leading the three horses. He stood before the teepee in silence. Would Grey Dove come out? Her father alone would decide. If the dowry was worthy he would give the order for her to go out from the teepee and sit in silence near the entrance, her face down. Her father ordered his two sons to take the stallion and the mare. It was a good sign. It meant that he could keep the colt.

"White Wolf waited in the falling darkness, but nobody came from the teepee. He was not refused, but he was not accepted. Several days were to pass before he was called to the teepee of Grey Dove. He had won the winsome Grey Dove. The horse trader returned during that time and had to go away disappointed and angry, but with many gifts for the inconvenience caused him."

"They were married soon after. What a happy gathering it was with so much feasting, singing and dancing! They were in the eyes of all a most ideal couple. Both were young, tall and strong. Grey Dove's beauty required a second look. It was not just her fine facial features, but a face that revealed humor as well as intelligence. White Wolf was unusually tall, very muscular, but also very lean. His bony facial features branded him a typical Sioux with wide, high cheekbones, straight nose, deepset black eyes and lean cheeks and chin. Few had heard him laugh. Few had seen his smile. In skirmishes with enemies, he was remembered for his fierceness."

"But Tya, what happened to them?"

She had groaned at his impatience. "It pains me still to think about it. I suppose I think about it every day. I will talk of it once. You have a right to know.

"When you were six your father was made chief. All chiefs have pipes made from the red stone. This red stone is sacred to all tribes and is found only to the southwest at the place we all call Pipe Stone near the Sisseton tribe. Your father and mother were to make the three-day journey to bring back the red stone for the ceremonial pipes. It was to be an easy journey. The sun was warm on the lush open prairie. This was friendly territory. Some days a few scattered herds of buffalo could be seen.

"The evening of their second day out was clear and warm. They stopped to eat and camp for the night. A faint breeze blew from the south. A tiny fire was enough to melt the tallow for mixing with the ground corn. Some dried venison and berries completed the meal. That night they slept under the stars with their horses grazing nearby.

"That clear night on the prairie turned cloudy, and the wind changed to the southwest. Cold rain started to fall in large drops before they were fully wakened. The large drops became hail while bolts of lightning flashed fire. Then the lightning and thunder was everywhere and they were surrounded by a rolling, raging night-storm.

"White Wolf ran for the horses which were being pelted with hail and were wild-eyed with fear. As one horse was untied from its stake it tugged wildly. He held on to it as it plunged in a circle. It kicked across the tether of the second horse, freeing it to run with the storm, and it was soon lost from sight. He finally calmed the other horse by covering its head with a blanket. There was no place to hide. The cold rain and hail would have to be endured.

"As he and your mother huddled against the scared animal they saw the flat grassland lit up like daylight. The thunder claps were loud and frequent. During the flashes an occasional buffalo was seen moving with the storm at a slow, lumbering gait, but veering away from them.

"Gradually a dull roar was heard, as a tornado sounds as it sucks up air and dust in its vortex. But tornadoes were seldom known of after dark. Suddenly there were more buffalo coming on both sides, racing in headlong flight. Crowded shoulder to shoulder nothing could stand in their way. White Wolf lifted Grey Dove onto the horse. Jumping on behind her he lashed his horse to outrun the bellowing herd. But so tightly was the horse crowded by the frantic animals that at times it was being moved bodily as part of the greater mass."

Tya stopped, her voice harsh, her hands clasped tightly.

"It was a race against death. How long could a horse with two heavy riders maintain its balance? Then it happened. A sharp dip in the terrain caused the horse to stumble. It went down on both front knees, and with the weight of the riders was unable to regain its balance. Both White Wolf and Grey Dove plunged over its head. He heard Grey Dove scream, but saw no trace of her. Somehow your father still had the rope in his hand, and somehow the horse righted itself. Half running, half being dragged, he felt he had a chance as long as he held on.

"Suddenly the herd changed direction as it came to a small stream bed. Ahead was a clump of willows. White Wolf on instinct jumped for the clump, set his heels and swung the horse about into safety. As he tied the horse securely he felt something in his back had snapped, and he fell to the ground in pain.

"The herd passed as quickly as it had appeared, but the wind and rain continued its fury. Finally, when it ended, he tried to stand. A pain like none he had ever experienced went through his spine. He felt nauseated. He tried again to rise, this time with all his will power. Again the horrible pain brought him to his knees. He found a short, heavy stick. Perhaps he could move while bent over. He must find Grey Dove.

"Dawn soon came. Leading the horse and leaning on the stick, he made his way back towards their campsite. On the open, trampled prairie he had to hunt before he found it. Here was a leather bundle covered with mud containing Grey Dove's personal belongings. He found the shreds of her blanket.

"It was light now and the prairie was a vast, empty place. With his back full of pain he hobbled downwind again. It was there that he found her muddy, crumpled body. It was easy to visualize what had happened. Hundreds of sharp hooves of buffalo weighing almost a ton each had broken her body and taken her life in moments. White Wolf, the fierce one in battle, wept as he cradled her body and wiped the mud and blood from her face. He would not leave her body here alone in this empty place. But how could he lift it on the horse? His pain would not allow him even to try. Taking two willow samplings, which he cut and dragged laboriously from the clump that had saved his life, he fashioned a travois by tying one to each side of the horse. The saplings angled to the ground, and between these he stretched the deerskin which had been thier bed. On it he placed the body. Walking bent over, he began his sad, slow journey to the nearest friendly camp of the Sissetons. Time had become unimportant.

"The sad news reached us before my son arrived with the body of his wife. The camp women joined him in his grief, as was their custom. There was a loud wailing and slashing of bodies interspersed with sad laments eulogizing the deceased. I retreated to my teepee while the other women came to console me. It was now my responsibility to comfort White Wolf and help in his healing."

Minnetaka had never seen Tya cry. Now the tears made streams down her weathered cheeks.

"Your father's pain would allow him little sleep. The medicine man spent an entire night calling on the spirits to heal and lift up this fallen warrior. Warm packs were applied. Pain-killing drugs of certain plants were administered. While each helped some the condition was not relieved. He would crouch and rock with pain.

In time he walked in a position bent far forward by using a very short cane. But a proud warrior could not go about like an old three-legged dog. He could not watch his companions prepare for and return from their hunting trips. Their stories, once so exciting, rankled deep in his stomach. He asked the Great Spirit to give him a sign. I sensed that he wanted to be with his beloved Grey Dove.

"That winter many of our band died of disease. White Wolf and you lived with me, of course, but you were too young to understand. I took care of him every day, though I knew he had lost all interest in life. One morning his forehead was hot. He coughed and sweated, then had chills. By evening he was having dreams. The medicine man came with his chants and potions and amulets, but could do nothing. The next morning he was cold, and in peace, as if he had decided that his time had come to enter the other world."

Tya's low voice had become labored with emotion. She had patted his head, conveying her sympathy and understanding.

"Tya, tell me, will I be a man like my father?"

"You are, my boy, just like your father."

8
The Buffalo Hunt

Three years passed. Minnetaka and Kiyi spent almost every day together. At sixteen, they were athletic young warriors, but untested in battle. Although they had developed their hunting skills, providing small game such as squirrels, rabbits and birds, and sometimes a deer, they had yet to prove themselves against buffalo — and against the Chippewa.

During the dark times of the long snows, they made bows of ironwood and arrows of red willow. The ironwood was peeled, dried until hardened like bone. Long evenings went by while they shaped and tested the bows for just the right tension when fully drawn. The last arrows were longer and heavier, made especially for a buffalo hunt. Flint arrowheads were not of their making; this was the special skill of older men of the tribe. But it took powerful arms to draw and hold steady the heavy hunting bows. Weight lifting and wrestling helped build the necessary muscle.

When another season of warm sun and green grass came, they were eager for adventure. To pass time they ran. Each day the two of them would race to the falls. The falls were formed by the sharp drop of the Redwood and Basswood Rivers as they plunged into the valley of the Minnesota one hundred feet below. Centuries of erosion by the rivers had cut eighty-foot gullies in the yellow clay, reminiscent of the rock canyons in the mountains of the far west.

It was their favorite playground, and a great natural shower bath. Thin saplings growing on the lower ledges leaned over a deep pool in one place. Standing above the saplings, the boys would dare each other to dive out and catch one near the top, then let it lower them to a position over the pool. From that dangling position they would drop into the eddying, white water. It was dangerous, but it was a skill that grew, another exercise to make their young bodies agile and their nerve disciplined.

At last, one day when the grasses above on the prairie were belly-high to a pony, Kiyi came running to Minnetaka's teepee. "We can go! My father said we can go on the buffalo hunt!"

Minnetaka in turn rushed to Tya. "I'm going with the buffalo hunters! Help me pack! I'll get my pony ready!"

She scowled at him as she skinned a young jack rabbit. "Now? Do you think the hunting party will leave in the late shadows? Huh! Yes, tend to Blackie. See to it that he's watered before dark. Blackie, like you, needs his rest, too."

They left the next morning, eight men and extra horses, and headed northwest toward the Lac Qui Parle prairie. At times they were out of sight of any tree or bush. But the fine weather, the lush grass, made it a keen experience, for they were in harmony with nature, and they knew that the buffalo would be seen within a day's journey.

Minnetaka had learned that buffalo herds had leaders. It was always the largest and wisest bull. The leader stood guard on high ground. He was comfortable only when he could see in every direction. He watched other groups. If they were quiet, he felt that his cows and calves were safe.

The hunters adjusted their strategy to their numbers and to the terrain. A scout would locate a small herd without alerting it. The hunting party would want to get as close as possible without detection. Upon a signal, the party would split and ride single file in two encircling arcs. Once the two arcs met, the one half would wheel around and all would be riding clockwise in a wide circle. This would gradually close into a smaller circle.

Often a herd would escape because a buffalo, even a yearling calf, could outrun a horse and rider. But usually there were several caught in the circle. The bulls and cows were a danger to be avoided. At this time of the year, the calves were the target. When game was abundant, quality became an option.

The second day out a scout came back. Minnetaka and Kiyi listened as he explained the encirclement. Having no seniority, they said nothing, but they could hardly conceal their excitement. They exchanged looks, eyes wide, grinning. This was their first buffalo hunt!

"Easy, Blackie, easy boy." Minnetaka's pony was a young stallion three years old, a gift from his uncle, Red Sun. He seemed to sense the excitement ahead. Tossing his head, switching his tail, he pranced in impatience.

All mounted, the scout gave the signal and the first riders rode off in opposite directions, Minnetaka and Kiyi were in the rear. They raced after their leader up and over a slight rise and were suddenly in full view of the target herd.

Minnetaka urged Blackie by giving him a kick in the ribs. The stallion raced across the prairie, his heavy breathing and pounding hooves as rapid as his rider's heartbeat.

"This is how it feels to be a man!" Minnetaka yelled, his words lost to the wind.

The circle was completed. If a calf came his way he must now be ready. Ready meant to maneuver Blackie as the calf darted and dodged to escape. Riding bareback with only a rope as a halter made this a test of horsemanship. Being thrown was always a possibility. To a youth it would be an embarassment not soon forgotten.

Minnetaka knew from his teaching that for a fatal shot with a bow and arrow one must be almost able to touch the animal. The object was to miss the ribs so that the arrow would reach the lungs. His first arrow shattered on a rib, he was certain. Disappointed but determined, he aimed and shot again. The second arrow nearly disappeared. He knew he had made a kill. The blood in the lungs would soon appear at the nostrils as bloody foam. Once the calf began to stagger, it would be over. Looking back he saw it wobble, then crumple in a heap.

He let out a wild cry of exultation. His first buffalo! Meat to be dried for the coming war with the Chippewa, a hide for many uses. Tya would be proud. And Kitsey. He would like her to know, even if he had not seen her for many moons. But it could not come from him. No, he could not tell her, but he would like her to know that he was a successful hunter, a provider. If only she could be there to share the heart and liver roasted over the fire!

After four days the hunt was over. From the prairies of the northwest, they started homeward, choosing to enter the Minnesota River Valley at the Granite Falls. This had been an unspoken hope on Minnetaka's mind. He could visualize their meat-laden ponies filing down to the encampment. She certainly would be there. Their affection for each other had grown with each yearly festival. Their close friends saw their relationship mature and seemed to accept that in time they would become man and wife.

9
Kitsey Captured

The Granite Falls tribe turned out enthusiastically as the hunting party came into camp. Minnetaka sought in vain for Kitsey. She was nowhere to be seen. He dismounted and moved about, desperate. Finally he saw a girl who he recognized as Kitsey's friend.

"Where is your friend, Kitsey?"

"She didn't come back. Didn't you hear?"

"No, I haven't heard anything!" He was impatient. "No, I've been away on a buffalo hunt."

"She went with a group north to the Four Lakes to fish — you know, in the Kandiyohi Lakes. A small band of Chippewa appeared out of nowhere. From Medayto, they say. There was no blood shed, but our people scattered in the woods, and when they came together again, she was missing. She liked to go walking alone. The fishing party came back here right away."

"But why just her?"

"Didn't you know her mother was Chippewa?"

"Chippewa? No."

The girl walked away, and he stood perplexed and unhappy.

The return home for Minnetaka was quiet and thoughtful. Kitsey was gone, a captive. Why had she not told him about being half-Chippewa? Why had it been a secret among everyone at the harvest festivals? He was resentful, then angry, then dazed. All he could think of was where she was, how she was. Was she in danger?

Kiyi on the other hand was exuberant, for he had also killed his first buffalo. He laughed and talked, recounting the details of the chase and his kill. Minnetaka joined in the conversation, but not in the same spirit. He had lost her. He was without hope, and nobody seemed to care or to understand. There was nothing he could do.

Tya was indeed proud of her grandson. She took the hide with satisfying grunts, and gave meat to those who had not been in the hunting party. It was the way of the Sioux. She even called a young boy and ordered him to take Blackie to the river to be washed and staked out in the grass. Today her grandson had become a man. It was good to have both the responsibility and the credit for his maturity. The entire band celebrated. There was much talk and laughter, but Minnetaka found himself enjoying the praise less and less. The sooner the day ended, the sooner he could think clearly about Kitsey and what had happened to her.

Even Tya seemed disinterested when he told her. "Half Chippewa, you say? Forget her. There are plenty of full-blooded Sioux maidens who would make you a good wife."

Later, as they ate a light supper, he was solemn. "Tya, remind me again why the Chippewa is our enemy. I'm trying to understand, and my head is a jumble."

Tya replied quickly, for she enjoyed the emotion of recounting the bitterness between the two nations, always hoping that the day would come for complete revenge, and that her only hope, her grandson, would help to fulfill the medicine mens' prophecies that the Chippewa would be driven from the Kandiyohi Lakes.

"You know they have taken our hunting and fishing lands from us and have killed many of our people. Once long ago our forefathers lived near the Great Lakes to the east. We were at peace with the Fox and Menomonie, our neighbors. There was enough game and fish for all.

"Then the Chippewa came from farther east, in canoes large and small. We welcomed them to hunt and fish during the fair season – but that was not enough for them. They were greedy. Soon they built wigwams and stayed. The game became scarce because there were too many people. Quarrels arose and there was war. Your grandfather was killed at that time. Our people scattered. We could not stand against them. So we moved west to Kathio on Lake Millacs, hoping to live in peace. Soon they came again, in the hundreds, and again we were driven out. Now they have all the wooded and lake areas to themselves. And what about us? We are scattered along a river that we never knew.

"We must hunt the prairies, the river valleys and small, timbered areas. But we lack lakes for fishing. The last lakes, as you know, were the Kandiyohi Lakes. Now they have taken them, too. To think it's already three years since you and I had to flee from Lake Mayto! And we've never found out what happened to our brave friends, High Hawk and Blue Feather."

"Never mind, Tya, the day will come. I promise you. But – tell me more, burn into me your memories so I will have our revenge."

She laughed harshly. "I think about your buffalo hunt. The Chippewa were never buffalo hunters, but they are so clever and learn quickly. It is said that from their main encampment on Medayto they go to the small prairies north of the Karishon River and often make kills even though they have no horses."

"But, Tya, no one can shoot the buffalo without a horse!"

She smiled. "You think you know everything from one hunt. You don't know the Chippewa. They find a water hole. After the rains, it becomes deep and muddy, and the animal becomes more helpless than on land. The Chippewa cover themselves with the same mud to cover their scent. Then the hunters surround the water hole with bowmen. When the animals are mired or drinking they rush in and shoot them while they struggle to flee.

They also drive buffalo, like deer, into the lakes. Even if they swim, they are easily overtaken by Chippewas in canoes."

"I'd rather shoot a buffalo riding Blackie. It's more exciting and Blackie shares in the chase. No canoe can do that."

"Don't underestimate your enemy! They have driven us out of our lands with their canoes. They carry them from one waterway to another. And canoes don't have to be fed and watered, remember that! Their portages are everywhere. Their large encampments are now at Lake Millacs and Leech Lake. Between these two camps are the Crow Wing Lakes. From there they can travel everywhere because most of the streams in the center of the

Upper Falls of Karishon
New London Townsite

northlands flow through these lakes and rivers to join the Mississippi."

"But how do they get to Lake Medayto?"

"There is a river that flows directly from Medayto east to the Mississippi. It is the middle fork of the Karishon River."

She took a piece of birch bark and sketched a crude map with a charred stick. "See here. It starts at Crow Lake, then flows south to Lake Monongalia. From there it winds among cedar islands and tumbles over the Upper Falls. It is a narrow stream until it reaches Nest Lake. After that it becomes wide as it empties into Medayto at the Lower Falls where the Chippewa now have their main camp. At the northeast side of Medayto it passes Loon Lake as it begins a winding route to the east, about three day's journey by canoe. There it joins the south fork of the Karishon. Not much further it joins the Mississippi."

"So – the Chippewa can come and go in three days by canoe."

"Yes, it's an easy journey. The Chippewa are shorter than the Sioux, but they are strong. They can paddle a canoe all day. With many paddling they move as fast as you can run."

Down the Karishon

Minnetaka jumped up. "I don't think I'll sleep tonight. Don't worry about me."

"Forget about her." Tya scowled.

"I can't. I'm going to talk to Kiyi."

Minnetaka spent the evening around a fire with his friends, mostly recalling the details of the buffalo hunt. There was much laughter and telling of stories. And, of course, there was talk and teasing about girls. It was as if nothing had happened to Kitsey; nobody mentioned her name. He grew angry with Kiyi first, then with the others. They were still little boys, he decided. And, without warning, he got up and left.

The moonlit night was good for running and being alone, so he climbed the bluffs above the camp. As he loped along the well-known paths, he shuddered, even though it was not chilly. If there was war this season, what would happen to her? His mind had glimpsed a scene that it dared not re-examine. It was of a massacre at the main camp of the Chippewa on Medayto, Kitsey caught up in the sweep of reckless killing as his people vented years of revenge against the enemy.

The running cleared his mind. His heart was pounding partly from the exertion, but also from the compelling need for an immediate decision. Somehow, he must get to Medayto. Alone. He would find Kitsey, but would she be friend or foe? It was clear he must take any risk to find the answer.

He stopped and looked up, panting. Here the world was lighted by the moon; here on other nights a million stars winked. Why did the Great Spirit keep its secrets from his children? It was easy to understand that the earth was their mother and all forms of life sucked at her bosom, but what about the heavens? How many stars were there? Why were they there? What brought the rain, the snow, the winds, the clouds? If the Great Spirit controlled all this, did it have time to hear him. Tya always said that he who was patient would receive a sign. What kind of sign? Where to look, where to wait, how to know? The scene never failed to fill him with awe. But the awe always changed to frustration. It was not enough to be a tiny spectator.

Minnetaka, in anguish, confronted the inscrutable moon. "There must be a life beyond this life. I ask the rolling thunder, but a blinding flash of lightning is the only reply. Is the Great Spirit my enemy? Am I just a spectator? Why must I ride a blind horse - facing backward, knowing where I have been, but not where I am going? Is the past the beginning? Does my father White Wolf and my mother Grey Dove wait for me? Oh, Great Spirit, listen that I may be worthy of thy grace."

It was time for sleep, but his mind was not ready for sleep. To sleep he must run until exhausted. There was solace in running. The prairie was firm underneath. The grass brushed his bare legs. Running became a rhythm without feeling or pain. One could run and be almost unconscious of any sensation.

He began to stumble from numbness to his limbs, and his chest burned. Suddenly there was a whirring noise from a low thicket nearby, and in the moonlight a small grey owl called softly. He stopped short, fell to the ground, and watched as it glistened briefly, then disappeared.

"Kitsey," he said harshly. "Kitsey."

He knew in that instant that she was all right. The Great Spirit had given him a sign, at last. But where exactly was she, and how had she been captured so easily? He lay down in the cool, damp grass and tried to think. Finally he slept.

Screech Owl - an Omen

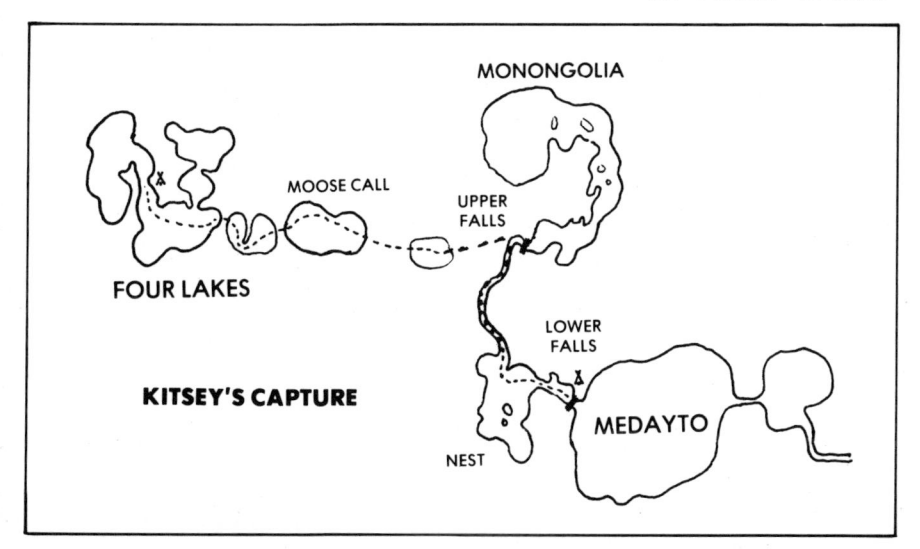

[Map showing MONONGOLIA, MOOSE CALL, UPPER FALLS, FOUR LAKES, LOWER FALLS, KITSEY'S CAPTURE, MEDAYTO, NEST]

Kitsey's capture had happened quite simply.

The trip to the Four Lakes was familiar to her. It was a long overland trail from the Granite Falls which she and several women had taken in the company of four hunters. They traveled in silence and worked in silence, for they had no wish to encounter the enemy. It was only to fish and to gather early berries.

The Four Lakes included four lakes in the rough shape of a clover leaf. In the center was a great, virgin woodland. It was unique to the area because any wooded area exposed to open prairie would eventually be set afire by the frequent fires. Some were set by hunters to drive and kill game. But here the great woods were surrounded by lakes and marshes and its trees had survived for hundreds of years.

It was a refreshing change for Kitsey as she walked alone in the cool moistness of the evening. The young trees strove upward for the sunlight needed for life. But as the small trees failed they guaranteed the success of the older trees. They, in turn, having shaded out all challengers, had the rich woodland soil to themselves. Each tree grew older, taller, and its crown became more dense. So dense that even the lower branches of the large trees were themsleves withered from lack of the precious sunshine.

The result was an inpenetrable umbrella of leaves that presented its top to the sun while underneath the shaded forest floor was moist, cool, dark and quiet. The chatter of a chipmunk rang loud, as did the scream of an alarmed bluejay invisible in the lofty tree tops.

It was not unusual for Kitsey to walk alone. She had worked hard with the other women. They had set their nets in a channel. The day's catch had been cleaned and were now being dried. The evening meal was over. It was dusk, and a cool walk along the east shore would give her a view of the sunset. As she walked along an ancient deer path, her thoughts went back to the young brave from the Red Wood Santee Camp. She knew after three years, of only the briefest of meetings, that he was the one she must have as a husband and father of her children. He was quiet, thoughtful – and yes, tall and handsome. He would not beat her or make her unhappy, she was certain of that. Oh, why could he not be here, at this moment, to share her peace and joy?

She stopped, hearing a strange sound. It was very near. There was a "tuck", then silence, and another "tuck." It was getting too dark to see. She then turned, she was in a hurry to reach the lakeshore. Suddenly there was a loud poofing sound followed by a whirring of wings. It startled her, but she saw nothing. Suddenly it was repeated. This time she saw a gray shadow sail off through the trees. It was her first encounter with a ruffed grouse, and she smiled thinking how silly it had been to be alarmed.

She moved on with an easy stride, reaching the lakeshore. The sun was now dropping out of sight. It would be cool sleeping. The clear sky promised another bright day.

The path led through a clump of brushy swamp willows. As she entered it, she saw a movement out of the corner of her eye. She turned abruptly and found herself face to face with a man and knew he was a Chippewa. Hearing a noise behind her, she saw a second man. She understood their signals for silence.

One held her while the other stuffed her mouth with a wad of soft leather. He then tied a soft strap across her mouth and behind her head. Fear and anger left her frustrated. Why did she wander off despite warnings from the Sioux hunters?

The trio kept to the deep woods. It was dark now. Suddenly they emerged on a sandy beach. They brought their canoe which had been hidden nearby. Each took a paddle, but first they tied Kitsey's wrists together and had her lie down in the craft. The stars were out, and there was no wind. As her captors paddled east towards the rising moon, she had no idea where she was being taken or for what reason. All that went through her mind was how careless she had been.

Unknown to her, their route took them through the narrows between the two Larger Lakes and across a short portage into Middle Lake. Another portage and they were on Moose Call Lake. There her captors chose to follow the north shore. In the high, wooded hills could be heard the occasional call of a wolf. Another less familiar sound was also heard in the distance. It was a heavy rumbling unlike anything Kitsey had heard before. The night air carried the sounds across the quiet water. The paddlers exchanged grunts and stopped paddling. The man in the forward position lifted a birch bark cone to his mouth. By blowing heavily a slow bawl was produced, ending with a series of coughs that seemed to carry a great distance.

In direct reply came a deep, chilling bawl from high up in the direction of Mount Toma. One of them grunted, "Oswego." The word was familiar, but its meaning escaped her. She thought of many animals, but this one was strange.

The second man said, "Oswego anamon." Then she remembered her childhood tongue – "Moose coming." She had never seen one because they were seldom seen in the Minnesota River Valley. They preferred the heavy woods, and the lakes and swamps of the Kandiyohi Lakes.

The two men whispered and laughed softly. Kitsey listened intently and understood that they were playing, like boys, pretending to be a cow moose with their call. Where a thin growth of bull rushes ringed the shore, the paddlers steered their canoe and stopped. They were in shallow water, a stone's throw from the shore.

The first paddler blew again the wail of a cow moose. The reply was instant, this time very near. They waited in silence. Soon the crackling of dry branches could be heard coming ever nearer. There was heavy breathing and grunting, but nothing to be seen in the darkness.

The Chippewa with the birch bark cone filled it quietly with water. Lifting it high above his head he poured it into the lake, imitating the sound of a urinating cow moose. It was a dangerous thing to do.

Here was the final signal to the bull, and it charged. Galloping in great leaps it hurled itself into the rushes, splashing, thrashing, turning in total confusion, expecting to find its amour.

The young men had had their fun. They and the canoe were in danger. One slapped the water with his paddle and yelled, "Ha-yee, ha-yee!" The moose stopped just short of them, sniffed, snorted in disbelief, and in a few great leaps wheeled about and was gone.

To Bear Lake was a mile-long portage. Another portage and they were at the Upper Falls of the middle fork of the Karishon River. They headed south to Nest lake, then east to their main camp at the Lower Falls at Lake Medayto. During the journey, Kitsey heard little conversation between the men. But she was surprised to recognize more Chippewa words. She was less alarmed than she had been at first, but being bound and gagged made her realize that there was no hope for escape. She was a prisoner, for reasons she could not understand. Was it because of her Chippewa mother? If so, why at this time?

Her mother, Red Bird, had been part of a small band of berry-pickers who had been surprised by a Sioux hunting party. She was sixteen and at that time lived at the small Chippewa encampment where the St. Croix flows into the Mississippi. One of the Sioux captors, an already-married brave named Big Elk, took her brutally as his second wife, dooming her to slavery.

Once at the Granite Falls Camp it was different. The old squaws were jealous and resentful. The leader of the hunting party came in for much condemnation. Red Bird was young and by any standard attractive. She had a quick step and an alert smile. Her daughter, Kitsey, was soon accepted by the children of her own age.

When Kitsey was old enough to understand, and wondered what had happened, the old Sioux squaws at the camp would only say that her mother had run away, and that was all right as far as they were concerned. One less Chippewa was just fine with them.

Meanwhile her captors were on the final lap of the canoe journey, Kitsey wept silently, wanting to wail. The restricting gag made her sick, her mouth was sore, and her wrists were chafed from rawhide. She stared up at the moon, ached inwardly, then thought of Minnetaka. Would she ever see either of them again? Moon, stars, Great Spirit, she thought, tell Minnetaka where his White Swan had flown – his Kitsey.

10
Council Of War

Minnetaka woke with a start, his entire body slow to respond after running and lying on the chilled earth. His head was clear nevertheless, and he recalled hearing the small owl in the darkness, then seeing it fly away in the moonlight. It was as if Kitsey had spoken to him. It was a true sign from the Great Spirit.

He knew now what he must do.

When he returned to camp he talked to no one, plunging into the river to bathe, then striding like the man he now was to his and Tya's teepee. When she looked up into his face, she said nothing, as if she knew what had passed during the night. She clucked and waited upon him with food. He was ravenous.

Only when he asked, "Where are all the men?", did she smile.

"In council ... for good reasons. If only you were not so impatient. No matter, you had to do what you had to do, my grandson. Go! You will not want to miss what they say."

Wiping his mouth, he leaped up and ran to the chief's teepee. All were seated there, grave, each speaking in turn as he approached.

"Now, I say!" an older warrior stated, slapping his thigh. "This bold move by the enemy is another insult to we Sioux ... especially because it was on historical Sioux lands!"

"Yes, it must be soon. We have waited three seasons." There was a babble, and Chief Grey Dog bade them to be silent. "Runners have come back. We are strong enough now. We have many horses, good weapons, trained warriors." He nodded to the man who had just spoken. "Crow Wing is right. Though the girl is half Chippewa, she was brought up a Sioux. It is not just for her that we must make war. It is because this is the final humiliation. What happens to a captive is not something we can avenge in itself. It is not

Grey Dog, Santee Chief

a rescue mission. She is yet another symbol of all that we have suffered from the Chippewa.

"All the chiefs are agreed. All the tribes will gather here for the great assault against the enemy at the Kandiyohi Lakes. We will make war ... and this time we will win!"

There was howling as men jumped up and danced to frantic drum beating. Nobody noticed Minnetaka in the background during the frenzy. But his chest swelled when he knew that it was Kitsey they spoke of. She had become a symbol. But — not rescue her? He pushed his way into the circle and held up his arms, calling for attention. Soon the noise subsided.

Since the buffalo hunt, Minnetaka's stature had increased. But they also remembered the plucky boy who had beaten the bully, Jotee. They would listen to Minnetaka, even the chiefs and the medicine man.

Head held high, he turned in a full circle, looking all of them in the eye, until he faced Grey Dog.

He spoke with conviction and passion: "Last night the Great Spirit gave me a sign through the girl I want as a wife, White Swan. She who was taken at the Four Lakes by the enemy. If I speak in a riddle, it is so. She who flies freely has her wings clipped. And yet ... her feathers fall marking the way. At the end of the way is the Great Tree of a thousand crows. The wingless white swan will defeat the crows and bring freedom to her kind."

There was murmuring and nodding. His eyes blazed.

"I, Minnetaka, have been given a sign. Heed it. I must go to White Swan. It will be dangerous. But ... I must go alone. The swan will reveal the weakness of the crows. And that will give us the victory!"

Again every man yelled approval. When they calmed down, Minnetaka addressed Chief Grey Dog: "I want permission to scout Lake Medayto, to find White Swan. Does anybody know how many wigwams are at the Lower Falls? Some say there are three camps on the lake. What about other camps ... on Lakes Manah and Koronis and Loon? At the Upper Falls near Monongalia? They are everywhere, we know that. But, how many?"

"We have scouted," Grey Dog grumbled.

"How many?" Minnetaka challenged. His muscles tensed, as he realized that he might be too bold.

"We are not sure." He looked up at Minnetaka. "You speak well for a youth. It is not enough to carry the spear, the bow and arrow, the tomahawk ... if you do not know the enemy's strength. You would go alone? No. Other scouts must go with you."

"Then I choose Kiyi and, yes, Yellow Bee and Weasel. Four will be enough. We will be gone no longer than six sunrises."

Grey Dog looked about. "Is it agreed?" There were no objections.

"Now ... if your hunting party was six and you came upon a Chippewa hunting party of four, would you attack?"

The youngest braves chanted, "Yes."

The chief's eyes sparkled. "Supposing the place you met was near Lake Medayto."

"Attack," said some. A few said, "No." Minnetaka was one who said no. He knew he was being tested.

"If two of your band were killed and three of the enemy were killed would you claim a victory?"

Nobody answered, not knowing his motive.

"Very well, if we were a war party of three hundred, half of our party on horses, should we attack a village of five hundred, including women and children?"

By now all the braves were silent and uncertain. The chief waved his hand, indicating they were dismissed. "Think about it," he said. "Think about your wives and children. We will talk again before battle.

Before he left, Minnetaka's arm was seized by Grey Dog. "Go in the morning with your friends. I trust in you. But do nothing foolish over the girl. She is only that ... a girl."

"I will do what is right," Minnetaka said. "I will do what is right for our people."

11
A Scouting Mission

Minnetaka and the other three young scouts left at dawn. They traveled with light provisions, not wanting to burden their horses in case they met an enemy force and had to escape. As they set out, Kiyi was talkative and light-hearted, as usual; so were the others. But Minnetaka had slept fitfully, his mind going over the route, and especially planning in detail how he would make contact with Kitsey.

Since Chief Grey Dog had given him authority, he assigned Kiyi to the next most responsible task to his own, that of the south and east shores of Lake Medayto, and the north shore of Lake Manah. To Yellow Bee was given the Karishon River north to Lake Monongalia. Weasel was to cover what was believed to be an unpopulated area from the High Lakes west and north to the Four Lakes. He knew that there were Chippewa on Koronis, and without a doubt on several other lakes and rivers north and east. He had been instructed by the chief not to extend their missions that far. They were to move swiftly in gathering the facts, then return. The messages were already being relayed to tribes up and down the river that the time had come to gather and strike.

They encountered nobody the first day, as expected. It was known that the Chippewa, satisfied with the riches of the Kandiyohi Lakes, had little interest in the smaller lakes to the south and west. That they could have scouts beyond their main camps, however, was a sober fact. So, Minnetaka was ever watchful when his friends seemed too lax.

To save time, they did not hunt that day, but ate the dried buffalo meat from the recent hunt, tended to their horses and moved quickly onward. By evening they were at the Wagonga chain of lakes which stretched eastward like a string of beads. No fire was built, and each took his turn at watch during the night.

Leaving the Wagonga area, they made their way in pre-dawn over the open prairie to the Teepee Lakes, which were the approach to the Kandiyohi Region. There they paused and rested on the crest of a small hill that overlooked the first lake. They named it Teepee Hill. The opposite wooded shore appeared to be an island. Looking at his birch bark map, Minnetaka knew they had arrived at the place known as Victory Island ... Robbins Island.

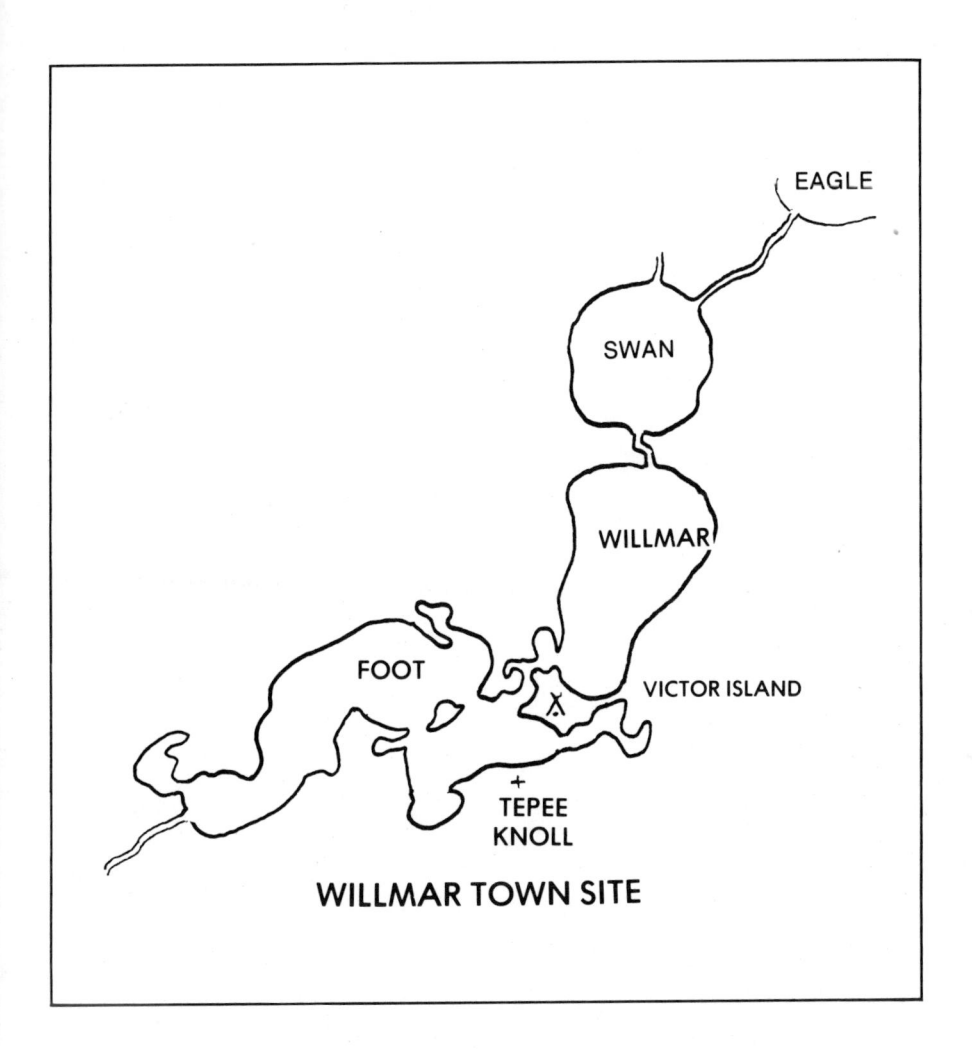

WILLMAR TOWN SITE

It was a peninsula, not an island. Many seasons ago it was a refuge for Sioux women and children during an attack by the Chippewas. The Chippewas made the mistake of assaulting the wooded peninsula, assuming it was lightly defended. Sioux hunters returning from the western prairies soon joined the attack, this time from the enemy's rear. It was a short savage encounter. The Sioux tell the tale often. The peninsula was thereafter known as Victory Island.

Minnetaka pointed. "There. There we will leave our horses and go on foot. I think the Chippewa are afraid of Victory Island. They have seldom been known to hunt or make camp nearby."

Again there was no fire, and they spoke in low voices, mindful that the hunters were also the hunted. In the late evening, traces of a ghostly mist hung over the lake. Minnetaka watched, enchanted by the serenity of the scene. Below him, small fish broke the surface and the silence with a barely audible "tup" as they sucked in small flies. Their green forms appeared and disappeared in the iridescent water. From a bare limb above came the alarmed scream and a flash of blue as a hooded kingfisher dove for its prey. And a great blue heron came gliding effortlessly, its image mirrored in the lake's still surface. As it neared the shore it dropped its gangly legs, banked its wings and settled into shallow water. The great bird dipped its head, then quickly threw it back as if enjoying the cleaning. It then stalked its evening meal.

Minnetaka was glad to have the first watch; he was not tired. Held by the beauty of the place, he felt that he was a privileged interloper. The moist air carried the subtle scent of earth and grass. It reached deep into his lungs, clearing his nostrils and sharpening his awareness. This was nature in its timeless balance, and he was a part of a never ending pageant of time.

Before the sun rose, each of the scouts was on his way with the warning from Minnetaka: "If you are captured, you will be tortured. Are you ready to sacrifice yourself for our people? Remember, if you reveal anything, you betray the entire Dakotah Nation. I am ready to kill – and to die, if necessary. If you do not feel the same, then it would be better if you took your horse and returned to the valley." He looked intently from one to another. Not one looked away or flinched. "Good. Then go. Chief Grey Dog said that we must come together again on the fifth morning – no longer. Whoever is not here then must stay behind or make his own way without a horse."

Point Lake Pass

Minnetaka made his way to Long Lake, then to the other small lakes to the northeast, keeping low in ravines and away from the crests of hills. From that point on he could expect to find the enemy anywhere. Berry-pickers, fishing and hunting parties could appear out of nowhere. He must not kill if possible, he must not be discovered.

Now for the first time, alone, he must draw upon all his knowledge, cunning and instinct for survival. Stealth, more than anything, guaranteed success. Every youth practiced it, every hunter and warrior took pride in it. He reflected; here was the test. It meant success or humiliating failure, or life itself. Impatience was the danger. He had reminded the other scouts of that. The old warriors and hunters had patience. For the young it was a difficult, oftimes dangerous, lesson to learn. He would need his four nights, so from this day on he would move only after sunset and sleep when possible during the day.

He knew that the portages were the closest routes between the lakes, if he could find them. He must. One at a time he would observe them from good vantage points. If the enemy had moved as far south as Eagle and Long Lakes, it was important to know.

Before the day ended, he had followed the high ground between Long and Point Lakes to observe any movement. There was none. By creeping to the high hills north of Eagle Lake, he could see the open prairie almost to the Medayto Prairie. There seemed to be no recent foot traffic that he could detect.

The wooded area he must penetrate was bordered by Lake Medayto on the east, the Karishon River on the north and Nest Lake on the west. Tya had simply given it the name, Big Woods. Once within it, his mission would focus on the main camp at the Lower Falls, the inlet — where the Karishon empties into the Medayto (Old Mill Site). It was an ideal camp site. And that was where he hoped to find Kitsey.

Eagle Lake Lookout

By nightfall, unchallenged, he was in the Big Woods, satisfied and weary. He gulped down food and made a bed for himself in a dense plum thicket. Tonight he must sleep, and be alert tomorrow.

As he was falling asleep, he remembered the one time he had been at Lake Medayto when a small boy. It was during the hot season, and all had looked forward after the long journey north to the cool water. Reaching the southwest corner of the lake, the entire party had waded in, leaving most of their clothes on. Even old Tya had waded in, waist high, and had come out dripping wet and laughing.

The boys were soon playing the game "Otter." One boy, the "Otter", must catch another. The latter then became "the Otter" and must tag another. It was done by diving underwater. This shore had a beautiful white sand beach, also a very distinct drop-off at waist depth. By standing at the drop-off one could dive into the dark water, see small fish eye-to-eye and feel the drop in temperature. It was an easy way for a good swimmer to escape the "Otter."

But, he was no longer a boy; he was now a man with a dangerous responsibility ahead. His thoughts turned to Kitsey, and he fell asleep thinking about her.

12
Kitsey In Captivity

And Kitsey was thinking about him as she tried again to sleep.

She was a curiosity in the Chippewa camp. Her dress, her speech, and her reserve – and yes, her attractive face and body all combined to make her an object of study. True, she was half Chippewa, but the imprint of Dakotah was upon her. To be Chippewa meant to be more open, fun-loving. But their way was not her way. She could not change.

Her serious demeanor was not without reason. She was, after all, in a strange place, a prisoner. She was neither trusted nor accepted. The work demanded was not a problem. She was young and strong, and teenage girls had leisure time. There were many older women for the hard work. The young girls were expected to learn by assisting, but drudgery could wait. It was as if the older squaws remembered the passing, all too quickly, of their maiden days. They alternated between tolerance and envy of the young generation.

Kitsey, by being modest, was soon accepted by a group of girls her age. As part of this group her freedom was extended to nearby camps, and to berry-picking jaunts and other unpredictable girls' pastimes.

She was told very directly that she was not really trusted by the older women. She was warned to make no attempt to escape; if she did, the result would be death. It was also explained that she would be protected and treated well. So, she was free to move about if she never wandered off alone.

The days were filled with activity much like that to which she was accustomed. But the nights were difficult. After a period of sleep, she would awaken suddenly. Lying awake, listening to the breathing of the other women, her mind would wander. With her whole life ahead of her, what could she hope for? Already she was a topic of conversation among the young braves. Others who looked at her were not so young. Fears for the future never left her. She was Dakotah, not Chippewa. Yet, she knew she had no control over her future. There was perhaps one small hope.

She was sure that Minnetaka knew and cared. She day-dreamed of him coming and taking her back home to the Granite Falls. She knew that was unrealistic. But − if he did come, how would she know?

Two old women in the camp kept small fires all night, usually to dry strips of meat and fish. Kitsey often talked to them when she was sleepless. She quickly re-learned much of the Chippewa language. One women was sullen and tight-lipped. The other was talkative, with a sense of humor and, within the limits of tribal custom, was inclined to be motherly. During these night vigils she became entranced with Medayto and its moods.

After being awakened by a clap of thunder one night she appeared from her wigwam. The air was fresh and cool, the sand underfoot was firm. A receding electrical storm hung over the lake, sending its lightning bolts downward in grotesque designs. With each flash coming from a different direction it lit varying mountainous cloud banks, each time from a different direction. It was a monumental display as each scene changed to the accompaniment of thunder, first from afar, then near, sometimes as if from the trees overhead. The dramatic display moved slowly away, its pyrotechnics mirrored in the calm lake which now seemed content to play a supportive role in the drama.

13
Enemy Territory

When Minnetaka awoke the following morning, it was raining softly, and the Big Woods was still. It was good, he thought, as he silently prepared himself for the long day and the long night ahead. This was perfect weather for spying. If he could learn the enemy numbers at the main Chippewa camp at the Lower Falls, and other camps nearby, then he could concentrate on his plan to find Kitsey. But his first duty was to his people, if they were to win their forthcoming war against the Chippewa.

Leaving his plum thicket, he retraced his route to the High Lakes, he climbed a tall tree, waited and watched intently. Again he looked east toward the Medayto Prairie and saw nothing but the long, waving grasses. Apparently the enemy was content; they felt no need to explore, fish or hunt farther south. The mist continued to drift down. Wet as he was, he felt safe. But now he must undertake the two most dangerous tasks: to scout the enemy main camp, and to find a place in that camp that was secure for the next three days.

It was dusk when he snaked his way through swamps and brush towards the Chippewa encampment at the Lower Falls. After clambering to the uppermost branches of a huge oak, he saw there were wigwams as far as he could see. He tried to count them. There had to be at least four hundred inhabitants. If there were other camps in the area, they were probably smaller – and that was Weasel's task, up the Karishon at Upper Falls. There was no doubt that this was the center, the main camp – and probably where Kitsey was being held captive.

Darkness was coming and he had to find a secure place, a base from which he could be near the Karishon and the well-used paths alongside it. He knew how precarious his position was; if he was caught, it would mean torture and death.

The Karishon between Medayto and Nest Lake was a slow wide river. The south bank dropped sharply. Its shoreline was made up of slight curves. The north bank was made up of deep curves forming islands, bays, and points. The Chippewa groups were spaced out along the south side. The groups of teepees were connected by foot paths often near the water's edge.

Minnetaka remembered Ghost Raven, the trapper, telling him of the area. His crude map showed the two shorelines. The north shore had a small island. There were foot paths on the north shore, but they were back from the river so as to avoid the points and bays.

If Minnetaka could find a way to advance through the heavy woods, keeping a distance from both of the camps, he could reach the river. It would be difficult to find. He remembered that Ghost Weasel had told him that the island was small, but stood out of the water higher than a tall man. It had a flat top with good sized trees. Towards Nest Lake were two points, but they were not high off the water. The little island could be an ideal observation point if it could conceal him. He would watch the foot paths on the south side, hoping to find Kitsey if she was in this camp and if she had freedom of movement. All was a question.

In the darkness of the woods he moved north towards the river. A dog barked. Minnetaka listened. It barked again. Then he heard the dog yelp. All became quiet. The odor of fish filled his nostrils. It meant he was close to a camp. He moved away and was at the river. Trees across the river could be on the island. He would swim the river.

It turned out to be the island. By digging a cave this night he could push the dirt into the river. Some dry leaves or grass would make the cave more comfortable. Some brush could conceal the opening. It would take much of the night to find the right location and to dig a cave. There should be time for a short sleep. He then must stay awake during the day to watch for Kitsey. He must also be ready to convey some signal to her.

But what signal? He caught himself assuming she would be receptive to his attempts at communication. She had no idea he was in the area. Yet, he seemed to sense that the night air carried sympathetic vibrations that attuned their minds, bodies and spirits together for all time. He was certain that she would see and interpret his sign. She would also eagerly hasten to reply. But how would she signal? What message would she try to convey? All of a sudden he shuddered. Suppose it was he who could not read, who could not comprehend, her earnest, maybe desperate attempt at communication. He felt his breathing quicken, his hands become moist. He was shaken in his confidence.

A vision flashed through his mind. He saw his beloved, miserable in the Chippewa camp, the squaws overworking her, the children teasing her, the braves leering at her, and the old men taking obscene liberties as she passed. All this and maybe much more. Kitsey could, for lack of any hope of freedom, consider such a life to be a burden impossible to bear.

But these things must be put out of his mind. His mind must be clear and active. He must think like a mature Dakotah warrior. This was the first test of his warrior status. He must cultivate caution and patience, draw on all his instinctive intelligence and training – find bravery if the moment demanded it.

The location of the cave was critical. It must be concealed from both sides of the river, and positioned to provide visibility both upstream and downstream.

Heavy brush at the river's edge made progress difficult, but he finally found a large tree that had toppled into the stream. Nearby he saw a rock split in layers. Using sections of it, he started digging the soft, moist earth beneath the clump of roots. He had to work swiftly, forgetting danger, until the task was completed. When there was barely enough room for concealment, he curled up and slept, waking at daybreak.

After eating hurriedly, for he had little appetite, he watched from a point where he could see the river paths. If he was lucky enough to see her, he would place a sign, a symbol, along the path to which only she would attach any significance. What would tell her that it was a sign from him? What could he leave? He considered his personal belongings: bow, arrows, knife, pouch, moccasins. No, all of them would be childshly plain to the enemy, even young women. Could he arrange twigs, or bunches of grass, in some design to catch her attention? No, these too would be visible. Suddenly he remembered their first meeting when they were diving for clams. Yes? He would arrange three hinged sets of clam shells in a half-circle on one side of the path. The number and arrangement of the shells might attract attention, but only Kitsey would attach any real significance to these commonplace objects.

Minnetaka visualized the next development. Supposing Kitsey saw the shells and was reminded of their first meeting. What would be her reaction? Would she pick them up or kick them off the path? He concluded that he must wait. He had not even seen her. He did not know if she was in the camp. Then he had another fear; what if she had decided to live with the Chippewa? Would she then expose him to capture, torture and death? No, she would never betray him.

He shifted his position from time to time. The sun was rising. Yet, there was no sign of activity on the path. He could hear the babble of voices from the camp. Canoes passed so close that he could hear the conversation, even though he could not understand. Dogs barked. Voices came closer, this time on land. He heard children laughing, and the gossiping voices of squaws, but the foliage was too dense, and he caught glimpses only of parts of bodies, parts of faces. If Kitsey was passing by, there was no way of knowing.

Disheartened, and weary from not enough sleep, he realized that he must remain in his cave. He would place his sign that night, and hope.

He waited until the middle of the night before leaving his cramped hiding place. Making his way stealthily to the edge of the Karishon, he slipped into the water, carrying only a knife. If he was discovered he would have to deal with his adversary at close range, in a manner that would cause no sound. But, it was unlikely, since there had been no suspicion of his presence thus far.

The river was cool and calm, and the moon had come through the patched sky. Frogs sang on all sides. An owl hooted at intervals. It was easy to forget that there was danger.

Diving nude under the clear water he saw the light grey sand shimmering in the moonlight. Large, silvery, river shiners sparkled as their bodies flashed in unison. His mind went back to their first meeting, under water. If she were only here. If only they could be together on just such an evening.

Finding the shells and arranging them near the path was easily accomplished. And now, to wait.

There was nothing to do but to return to his cave beneath the tree roots and sleep again. He could detect the fires from the camp and the smell of drying fish. The smoke hung in the still air, appetizingly, reminding him to eat. He gnawed on the dry buffalo meat before unwrapping one of the small pouches prepared by Tya which contained dried, ripe plums and hazel nuts, preserved by a coating of bear fat. Having eaten, having left his sign, he slept.

He awoke at intervals during the night. The leaves were cold and damp against his skin. Peering out from the cave, he saw the moon had disappeared. All was quiet. Somewhere nearby he heard the thin squeak of a mink. Again all was quiet.

Suddenly there was an explosion. It was like an isolated clap of thunder, like a huge boulder plunging into the water near him. Those in the camp must have heard the same sound. He shivered. Could it mean that his hiding place had been discovered? Were the Chippewa trying to flush him out with some frightening act? He held his breath. All was silent.

Then the sound was repeated, this time farther away. There was something familiar now; he had heard it before, as a child. Ah – an alarm sounded by a male beaver as it lifted its broad, flat tail and pounded the surface of the water. He smiled to himself, feeling foolish.

He slept, fitfully, until dawn. Once more he watched and listened as Chippewa women and children trod the river path. The shells were there, waiting. He was waiting. But he saw no sign of her through the leaves.

It was not until after midnight that he dared creep near enough to the path to see. The clams were not there. Was he looking in the right place? Yes. He held his breath. There was one. Being cautious, his fingers sought out the other clam shells. They were there. Each had been turned over, each in an exactly straight line. His fingers lingered on them. There was no doubt that it was she who had found them, and was now returning the sign. Closing his eyes and clenching his hands, he wondered what her thoughts were. Oh, she knew he was there. But how would she return the communication? It was now up to her. He had to be alert.

Kitsey had been with a group of girls to catch turtles. The turtles were a summer delicacy. They went every day to wade waist-deep in the grassy swamp bordering Nest Lake. But they had to capture the turtles underwater. Kitsey had her own technique. First, she swam with her eyes always open; second, she kept her body almost flat along the bottom, digging her toes into the sand to propel herself forward with her strong legs.

It was on the return trip, as she was walking the well-trodden trail along the south side of the river, that something caught her eye. The other girls were talking and laughing.

The Hidden Cave

She saw the three clam shells as if they were staring at her. She felt fear immediately. Did the other girls see them? Did they notice any change in her face? Shells would not attract much notice, but three meant there was some purpose.

She decided that if an explanation was needed she could suggest that the children may have been playing there. Meanwhile, she could feel the conviction rising in her mind that the shells spoke to her alone.

Quickly, she set down her sack of turtles and said, "I need a clam shell. I saw one back there. Please wait for me." She ran back and quickly turned over the three shells, placing them in a straight line. "Oh, it wasn't the right size," she said. "I want one to make a hole in to draw my hair through while I swim." None showed concern.

It was a sleepless night for her. There was doubt, there was hope, there was love, there was the chance for freedom. All depended on the clamshells on the trail. In the entire camp, it was only she who lay awake, eyes wide open.

But she did sleep at last, and another dawn came with the sound of male robins beginning their cheerful warbles, telling all birdom of territories, mates and their young. The sun appeared above the eastern shore of Lake Medayto. The camp came to life, fires were started, smoke wafted up through the trees. From everywhere children and dogs appeared to frolic in the water among the huge rocks. And Kitsey came forth, knowing that on this bright, warm day Minnetaka was waiting somewhere not far away.

She was given orders which she quickly obeyed; to bring fresh, dried grass for the wigwam, to fetch water from the river, and dry branches for the fire. But today the tasks were easy. She would travel the path along the south shore as usual and would hope for another sign.

14
The Meeting

The evening came slowly. Minnetaka's thoughts wavered between despair, losing all confidence in his daring plan and his own courage and craftiness. The late sun was slow to sink beyond the horizon. Dusk followed, but Minnetaka needed total darkness to conceal his plan. The middle of the night would hopefully find the enemy camp asleep.

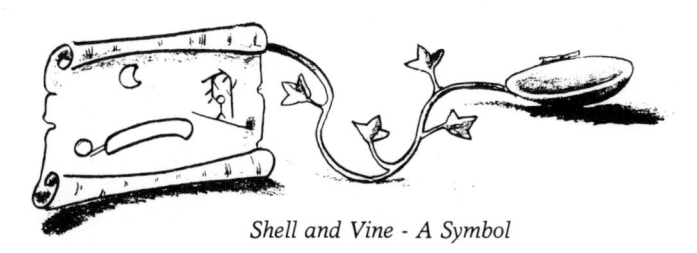

Shell and Vine - A Symbol

His plan, simple and daring in its concept, would start with a message to Kitsey. It would be in the form of a crude drawing with these symbols: A moon indicating nighttime. A canoe denoting the mode of travel. A drooping willow tree as the rendezvous, and a swimmer guiding an overturned canoe. These symbols would be drawn on the inside curl of birch bark and would be hidden near the trail. A single clam shell would attract Kitsey's attention. She would discover that the clam shell was attached to a small green vine that leads to the concealed sketch.

The plan, if successful, would unfold by Minnetaka stealing a canoe up river. He would guide it in its overturned position down stream. Upon reaching the overhanging yellow willow tree he would then guide the canoe under its branches. At this point, if Kitsey had read the symbolic sketch, she would be waiting. They would then glide downstream over the gentle falls out into the Lake Medayto to freedom.

He slipped into the river wearing only a breech cloth. Keeping close to the bank he swam along as smoothly as a muskrat until he came to a beach above the falls with many overturned canoes. It was simple to pull one into the water and retrace his route to the toppled tree. He was now committed to his desperate gamble; he no longer weighed the consequences of failure. His total concentration was one of being quiet, moving slowly.

The moon for the moment was clear and bright. He felt as if eyes were watching from the shore, from the trees. How quickly an alarm could be sounded. It could be launched and be upon him immediately. But he had confidence in his plan, and his own stealth. His training as White Wolf's son would see him through.

The Plan Begins

By the time he approached the overhanging tree, his senses were sharply alert, his skin tingled in the cool water, and his quick breathing was measured and even. His ears strained for sounds of danger, but all was quiet except for the sound of a screech owl — and that was his spirit-brother - a good omen.

To keep the overturned canoe from becoming entangled in the leaning tree branches, he treaded water and maneuvered it from moonlight into the shadow of the overhanging willow tree. Another hoot of the owl sounded closer by, and then a rustling in the blackness. He felt the canoe tilt slightly. She had understood the sketch. In a moment Kitsey was swimming silently at his side, as if by some miracle. He let go of a branch and let the canoe drift. As a wispy cloud passed across the moon, he could see her white teeth and a smile of shared elation.

Soon they were at the falls. Anyone watching from either bank would easily notice movement, but only the old squaws tending the fires were visible. The current pulled the canoe ever faster, and they were now at the point where it would carry them down the falls to the lake.

Minnetaka tapped Kitsey gently, signaling that they should take a deep breath, hold it and keep their heads underwater. Suddenly they were in a mad swirl of bubbles. The canoe was a bucking horse. Along with it, they were slammed against the rocks, but they held tightly, their young, supple bodies absorbing the bruises. Between the two of them they managed to keep the canoe in a straight line as they cascaded down into the peaceful flowage and out into Medayto.

Once they were far enough from shore, they righted the canoe and unlashed the paddles. Kitsey leaned forward in the water, her face close to his, still smiling, and imitated the little screech owl. It was their good omen. He smiled back, hardly believing that she was there.

15
Ecstacy and Pain

Laughing softly, trying not to giggle, they were at last able to climb into the canoe and paddle along the north shore by her direction. There they secured it in sparse rushes along a shallow sand bar. As if reading each other's minds, they entered the water under the full moon. In tandem, they imitated the graceful, gliding fish that flashed their silver sides alongside them.

Following her, Minnetaka slid off the rocky dropoff deeper in the emerald green world spotted with huge, brown crusted rocks. She pointed ahead. Swimming with rhythm and skill, she came to a place where she stood in waist-deep water, a sandbar. When he joined her they embraced at last, their glossy heads pressed together, their warm, wet flesh as one.

The Night of Magic

Suddenly Minnetaka pulled away. "Are you Chippewa or Dakotah?"

"Tonight," she said in their language, "we must think only of tonight." She threw back her head and laughed. "You are brave, but such a boy! Do you think I would risk my life ... like this ... if I were Chippewa?"

He was taken aback by her shift in moods. "I had to know."

"That was the only reason you came here to risk your life?"

"No ... to spy. Our people will come back."

"War?"

It was the moment he had feared. "Yes. We will make war within another moon."

"Oh, my beloved! Nothing can happen to me now ... now that I know you will return."

"There will be a massacre."

She nodded and held his hand against her cheek.

"What will you do?"

"Do not worry. I will know of your coming. Perhaps there will be a parley. Do our people come in great numbers?"

"Yes, twice as many as the Chippewa."

She drew back. "You know how many there are here among the Kandiyohi Lakes?"

"I have counted the wigwams in your camp."

"Oh. And what about the new camps at Nest Lake, and those above the Upper Falls, all those at the outlet of Medayto?"

"There are other scouts. I must meet them at another sunrise."

"Tell your chiefs to beware. The enemy is well-armed. They have many canoes."

"Yes, I will. But the time has come when we must drive them out, forever."

They were silent for a few moments. Then she smiled again. "As I said, we must think only of tonight." With that, she dove underwater with the liquid grace of an otter and disappeared. When she reappeared, he followed. It was an invitation to fulfill in the exquisite detail the magic of this time and place.

They shifted from the efficient crawl to a leisurely backstroke. It gave them the opportunity to set a relaxed pace. It spread the depths of the endless universe above them. Minnetaka watched as the bright moon caught in reflection the flow of tiny bubbles sweeping around her body leaving a trail of swirls behind.

Minnetaka pondered her strange appeal. Why was she so unique of all living creatures? Was it her vibrant response to life, to the tiniest detail of each fleeting moment?

He found some parallel in a young doe with her first pair of fawns. She was a part of the forest pattern of peace and quiet, of light and shade, of tender motherhood one minute and fearless defender the next.

Kitsey, like most creatures of the forest, was able to interact with its many facets, its many moods. No sight, sound, waft of subtle odor passed unnoticed. It was this wild creature alertness of hers that enchanted him. He could sense her parallel reaction to a rising fish in a quiet water, the quick examination of brilliant orange mushrooms pushing through the dry mat of leaves of the forest floor in spring. Her effortless stride as she walked ahead along a narrow trail, her grace and strength, combined with the mystique of her young body, and her ability to focus her vibrant being on making her chosen mate happy beyond description. He closed his eyes to picture each day with her at his side. He tried to picture a life without her. His mind rejected the picture like the mouth ejects a bitter plum. Lost was his freedom to choose. Either his world would be full of her sunshine and beauty or he would live a half-life in the overcast monochrome of a lonely exile.

As Minnetaka approached maturity he sensed that he needed someone to share his honors, his hopes and his fears.

He subconsciously welcomed manhood. There was new vitality in his being. Life came into sharper focus.

He now sought knowledge, strength, and growth.

He sought companionship and approval of other men.

He now demanded the utmost of himself.

He now assumed leadership over other boys.

He noticed that women now took notice of him.

He avoided women that made advances.

Subconsciously he sought a woman he could conquer - someone he could own, someone he could talk with, depend on, and trust without reservation.

He felt a need for somebody who would share in his success as well as his failures. There was only one, it was Kitsey.

Kitsey felt the stimulation of the cool lake, but she was warmed within by the knowledge that under the enigmatic moon was another human being who wanted her. Not merely because she had said she was Dakotah, not just because she was beautiful, not because she had worldly possessions. No, just because he had declared that his life would not be complete without her.

It was as simple as two lovers discovering the pristine beauty in the heart of a flower, each somehow perceiving the delicate impact upon each other. This moment was fleeting in its poignancy and beauty, as delicate as the blossoms, and it would be preserved in their memories as something sacred. It was a one-time - first-time moment sharing a virgin experience, never to be repeated.

Minnetaka pleaded, "Kitsey, come with me - to your home on the Minnesota with your friends - with me." "War is coming. It is safer for you if you are with the Sioux. By daylight, we can be near the Wagonga chain."

"Yes, I would be safer," she replied. "I, too, feel the war drums. They throb in my head as I try to sleep. I have a vision that keeps recurring. I am always alone in the dark storm encircled by huge trees. The wind is in the high trees. The trees bend towards me. Then thunder rolls and lightning flashes all around me, but I am not harmed."

Kitsey continued, "Sometimes the waning sun breaks out from behind the retreating clouds. Birds renew their singing, the rain glistens on the leaves, the world is at peace.

"Other times, the storm clouds close in, lightning flashes and human screams are heard above the angry thunder. I run among the dying bodies searching for a familiar face, but I cannot see clearly for friend and foe are all alike.

"I have asked the medicine man to interpret my dreams, but he says he cannot interpret a woman's dream. He said the Mandans have a man and wife who are both medicine healers and readers. He advised me to keep busy with camp chores.

"I talked to him a second time. This time he listened carefully. Then he said, 'Be patient, look for other signs. The symbols appear to center on you. The storm may symbolize the coming battle, the bending trees may be the opposing warriors.'

"Since that time, I have thought of nothing else. I do not know how or why I am involved in future events, but I am sure I am appointed by the Great Spirit to help bring peace. It is peace that will bring you and me back together. For this, I must return to the camp of the enemy to await the unfolding of events. My thoughts will be always with you."

Instead of returning to where they had left the canoe, Kitsey swam towards the low-lying shore due east of the falls. There she could cross in the protection of the woods, and enter the camp without being noticed.

Minnetaka waited until he was sure she was back in camp. He wondered if she had been missed. But there was no sound of angry, raised voices. Relieved, he wasted no time in going to his canoe and setting out across the lake southwest. Dawn was on his heels. He drove the padddles deep. Their rhythm gave expression to his new-found energy.

16
War Council

By the time he returned to Victory Island, the sky was pale blue and pink with another dawn. As he trotted towards his rendezvous he felt no weariness. The long swim, the reunion with Kitsey, had stimulated his mind and body, leaving him with a tingling sense of well-being. But there was the gnawing uncertainty of what would happen within another moon. True, he was facing manhood, but yet he was a boy. What would the future hold? Did he have any control over it?

Blackie and the other horses were in good shape, just restless from their confinement. So were Kiyi, Yellow Bee and Weasel. All had accomplished their missions and were eager to report to the Dakotah chiefs who must already be gathering with their warriors to form the long-awaited war party.

In high spirits they rode south over the prairie toward the Minnesota River Valley, confident as only youth can be, knowing that the information they were bringing would help assure ultimate victory for their people.

When Minnetaka and his friends arrived at the bluffs overlooking the Redwood Falls they stopped, amazed. A cloud of dust hung over the valley as hundreds of warriors spurred their ponies toward a growing encampment. They looked at one another and grinned. Minnetaka let out a shrill whoop, and the others joined in. They rode their horses in a circle, as if in a dance, yelling and slapping each other on the backs.

"It's finally happening!" Minnetaka cried. "Look, Kiyi!" He pointed. "There ... coming from the east ... they must be Wanamingoes and Winnebagoes!" Blackie reared up, as if infected by the excitement.

"Yes!" Kiyi shouted. "There ... to the west! See them? The Wahpetons and Sissetons! What a sight!"

"Look at all the teepees," Weasel said. "There must be hundreds."

Minnetaka strained his eyes, shading his brow from the sun. "They can't all be ours."

Yellow Bee, who made a study of symbolism, was smug. "Anybody can see that some teepees are Ponca, some Ogallalas."

Kiyi was impressed. "From that far away? From the Niobrara River?"

Yellow Bee nodded. "Theirs are the Palomino ponies. Not that they're any better than ours."

"What does it matter?" Minnetaka looked from one to another. "At last! We are one nation!" He let out another shrill whoop, whacked Blackie smartly on the rump and galloped down a worn ravine path.

Boys that they were, they almost trampled children, squaws, dogs, and the stretched hides drying in the sun. There were screams in their wild wake, then clenched fists and fury. But they were too exuberant to notice, finally wheeling about in a circle before chief Grey Dog's teepee. All leaped off their horses, giving them to eager little boys to take away to the river for a much-needed wash and rest.

Recognizing now who the brash intruders were, the people of the Red Wood Santee rushed upon them laughing and screaming. They were heroes! Tya waited on the perimeter before she threw herself upon Minnetaka, idolizing him, her mouth wide in an almost toothless welcome.

Chief Grey Dog appeared. His flinty eyes betrayed satisfaction, but his craggy face showed no emotion.

"So ... you've all come back. That's good, if the mission has been accomplished. If it was to chase does in the woods, then it does nothing for us." He looked intently at Minnetaka. "Are you ready to report?"

"I am."

"Tonight, then. All the Dakotah chiefs will be here, my guests for feasting and dancing. You're a very proud son of White Wolf. Don't be too proud. At your age, there is much to learn."

"I have learned much," Minnetaka said, looking him in the eye. "I know I have much yet to learn, but there is no man, Dakotah or Chippewa, who can call me a boy. I am now a man, a warrior."

Grey Dog nodded, turned, and went back into his teepee.

The multi-tribal council that night was a sight and an experience Minnetaka would never forget. There were so many chiefs, medicine men, and seasoned warriors that it made him feel little and insecure. And yet, he and his scouts had the crucial information, the most recent news, about the Chippewa forces in the Kandiyohi Lakes. This was a simple report: to state the facts and figures.

As he came forth into the fire-lit circle, he turned and looked from one burnished, grave face to another, impressed but not showing it. The chiefs with their full regalia of feathered headdresses, elaborate necklaces, soft elk tunics and breeches commanded respect.

"I am Bear Tooth of the Poncas," a deep voice boomed. "We have no time to waste. How many of the enemy are at Lake Medayto?"

He told them about the main camp, the hub, then he had Kiyi report on the other settlements, especially on the north shore, and a small camp at the outlet leading to Loon Lake. Bear Tooth and the others were satisfied.

"What of the Karishon River and north?" This time it was Chief Oak Leaf. "Do they have many at the Upper Falls?"

"No," Yellow Bee said. "Only a few to fish. They go upriver for a few days, then return. There are no permanent camps."

Weasel reported that the Four Lakes and the High Lakes were uninhabited except for a few who hunted and fished. He had watched their portages carefully.

In rapid fire, they were asked about more numbers – canoes, food caches, paths, portages, women, children, captives, weapons. Minnetaka became impatient.

"We have told all there is to know. Now, do you realize that the Chippewa are in the deep woods? Our horses are of no use once we leave the prairie. And they have their canoes. We'll have to fight them from tree to tree, hand to hand." Minnetaka replied.

"Should we parley?" someone asked.

"Parley? Give away our chance to surprise and kill them all?" It was a warrior of another tribe, a fiery, eager man. "Should we let them get away to breed more of their kind?"

Chief Grey Dog, the eldest, shook his head. "Shedding blood is not the only way. All we want is our sacred lakes. If they leave in peace, never to come back, then we have won the victory."

"I agree!" Minnetaka said loudly.

Several chiefs sat back and glared at him.

"Oh, he speaks out of love!" It was the firebrand again. "I'm Jotee ... remember me, Santee gopher?" He jumped to his feet, confronting Minnetaka. "You tripped me and pushed me into the river."

There was a loud murmur, and protesting.

Jotee, however, had the audience at the moment. "Did he tell you why he went to Lake Medayto? Did he? It was more to find a Chippewa bitch than to find out the strength of the enemy! Who knows what he would do for her. He might even have betrayed us!"

Minnetaka was stupefied, then mad with anger. It was simple reflex which made him draw his knife and attack Jotee, to slit his throat – but he was seized and held back, wrestled to the ground.

As he lay there, panting, he heard the chiefs condemn Jotee and banish him.

"What about the girl?" Grey Dog asked, once Jotee had been removed. "Did you see her?"

"I saw her. She is Dakotah, never fear. If I thought otherwise, I would have killed her."

"Enough," Grey Dog said, with his usual wave of the hand. "We are satisfied, aren't we?" There was no dissent. "Good. Then let us prepare for the battle."

Since dawn the squaws of the Santee, as well as those of the visiting tribes, had been preparing and delivering food for their men.

Tya brought Minnetaka his big black stallion. She carried a bag filled with dried meat, dried fish, nuts and berries. As he prepared to mount, she walked behind him and muttered, "Remember, after this battle the enemy will still live. Our nation will also live ... and you must live, too" It was enough. She was reminding him that his life was precious to her and that war would not really settle anything permanently.

The war party of approximately five hundred and fifty was now mounted and ready. The ponies, sensing the excitement, pranced in circles and reared up with hooves pawing the air, the stallions always ready to kick or bite one another should one get too close. The dusty scene was ablaze with color. The general, circular movement of the panorama had at its vortex the tribal chiefs in feathered headdress who now with a mighty war whoop for victory drove their steeds at full speed up the narrow draws to the upper rim of the valley. There in full silhouette they formed ranks against the cerulean blue sky. With another war whoop of full-throated unison they headed north to the Lake Regions.

Their routes, while generally following stream beds, were on solid ground. The high hills were avoided because a lone enemy scout could observe at a great distance. There was little danger of attack by ambush, but scouts were already far ahead, climbing any promontory to watch for movement. They were regarded as a shield, each protecting a small sphere along the main trail the war party was traveling. The pace was brisk, the mood elated but still serious.

Minnetaka rode close behind the assembled chiefs at the request of Grey Dog. It was an honor. Blackie was eager, but it would be impudent of him to ride ahead. Conversation was held to a minimum, the chiefs talking among themselves, giving precise directions when needed by hand signals that all had known since childhood.

Studying the rhythmic nod of his horse's head, Minnetaka felt himself as a link in a chain. His personal freedom was surrendered to a higher authority. The tribe needed his ability, but no more than that of any other. He was pledging his life to a cause that was greater than his own life. He must be worthy. He must now be ready to justify his abilities, his gifts as a warrior, by bringing victory on the battlefield and peace and security for his family and the tribe. If this meant taking the life of any enemy by his own hand he must be ready. When the moment came he must be ready, like the spring of a trap, to execute in a fatal flash. To himself he muttered, "I will be ready to act, I will be ready ... I will, I will."

They stopped for the night to rest themselves and their horses at Lake Mayto. The area was more water than land, marshes seeming to lead one into another and eventually becoming part of the bigger bodies of water, especially the namesakes of the region, the Big and Little Kandiyohi Lakes. The Santee chiefs knew the patterns of these wet areas and the best way through them. This season the water level was normal and ideal, and they made rapid progress after the brief stop.

Again on the move at daylight, they arrived at the Teepee Lakes and Victory Island. There they set up their tribal encampments and tethered their horses. There were the painted ponies with large patches of contrasting black, white and brown. There were the dun-colored buckskins with the dark brown feet, tail and mane. The copper-colored Palominos were much admired and coveted. The stallions, always a problem, kicked and bit until separated from each other and from the mares. This did not keep them from issuing their high-pitched screams of defiance to other stallions and a muted, throaty neigh for the benefit of the mares.

Their approach, from this point on, would be almost impossible to keep secret from the enemy. But so far there had been no sign of the Chippewa. Many fires were lighted, as if in defiance, and all gathered in a great circle. The chiefs were seated with all others standing or kneeling to the rear. It was the final conference.

Minnetaka stepped to the side of Lame Deer of the Granite Falls Santee and asked in a whisper, "What happens to the women and children in a fight to the death?"

The reply he got hit him like a whip. "It is the women who produce the bad seed which have for countless years murdered our people. It is easier to kill cows and calves than to kill the bulls."

He had known this all along, heard it all his life, yet found it hard to believe. His mind raced. He stared with fixed eyes at the great fire at the center of the circle. The voices of the speakers seemed far away.

What will happen to Kitsey? For a moment he saw bodies, slashed and bloody, heard screams of horror, screams of victory, then crying and weeping. He tried to control his agitation, hoping nobody would notice, and forced himself to listen to the chiefs' discussion. By concentrating, he put it out of his mind.

Each chief of the separate tribes had a chance to speak, but all had already pledged their approval of the battle plan. This was out of respect for Grey Dog who was known for his wisdom and caution. The pipe was passed solemnly to seal their unity. This was the Dakotah Nation at its zenith.

There were still questions about communication, tactics, even pursuit. Pursuit beyond Lake Medayto was ruled out. It would be dangerous with the Chippewa having the advantage of their swift canoes. Lake Koronis, though not far, was really on the fringe of the Kandiyohi Lakes. If the enemy came no closer than that in the future, there might be a buffer zone between the two tribes.

To make certain that every chief, every warrior, understood the plan, Little Bear, a nephew of Grey Dog distributed birch bark maps to each leader, then reviewed the charcoal directions:

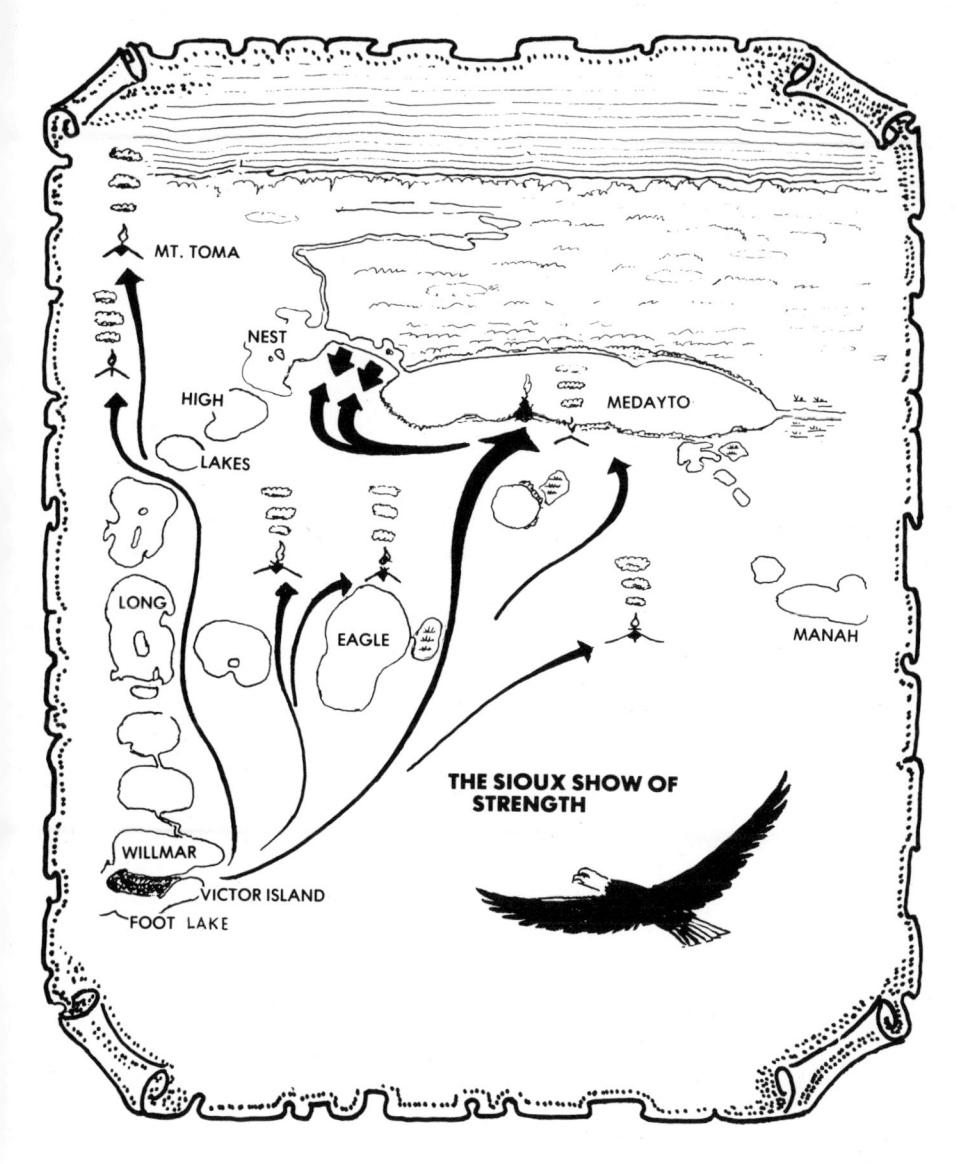

Map labels: MT. TOMA, NEST, HIGH LAKES, MEDAYTO, LONG, EAGLE, MANAH, WILLMAR, VICTOR ISLAND, FOOT LAKE

THE SIOUX SHOW OF STRENGTH

"The center prong represents our main force under Grey Dog. Notice that when we leave this camp and proceed north, the flanks will move east and west of Eagle Lake. Our central rallying point will be the woods north of Elkhorn Lake." He paused and looked about. "It is wise to have a gathering place whether in victory or defeat. Otherwise, we would be disorganized and scattered. If lost or wounded we return to this area.

"Our main forces will be gradually encircling the enemy that is now concentrated at the Lower Falls of the Karishon and upriver to Nest Lake. If they choose to do battle we have them surrounded and outnumbered. If they retreat, it must be by canoe by way of the Karishon flowing east from

Medayto. Once their large numbers are water-borne, there is nothing we can do. Many others may simply vanish into the deep woods north of Medayto and make their way to Koronis and in time north to the Sauk River.

"All signal fires will wait until the black smoke rises at the Eagle Lake Lookout. When all fires are making white smoke we are showing our strength. The attack is considered underway when the main fire is black smoke. There is only one objective after that ... to drive the enemy out of our lakes!"

The heavy silence was broken by wild shouting. Little Bear raised his arms and turned full circle.

"Today," he continued, "our advance scouts occupy every high point in every direction we intend to move. Yes, the Chippewa probably know we are here, but they have no idea of our great strength. Now, does any man wish to speak?"

Chief Grey Dog arose slowly; he was getting arthritic, but he still was athletic and commanding. He walked stiffly to the center of the great circle.

"You, my brothers, honor us this day. Tomorrow we plan to confront our common enemy on the very grounds made sacred by the blood of our ancestors. My own father, my sister, were killed many moons ago on the Nest Lake Islands. Outnumbered, they were all killed, their bodies hidden ... most likely in the lake itself. It is only one of many savage acts unavenged. Tomorrow my revenge ... our revenge may come. If I die on this mission, I have accomplished what I set out do do. I will die in peace."

Like the other chiefs, he was in full regalia. His eagle feather bonnet and weasel tail stole piece told of his accomplishments. His feathered war spear attested to his bravery in battle, each feather with its dyed markings a trophy of past years. To Minnetaka, it was history and legend come together.

Grey Dog sat down. There was nothing more to be said.

There was feasting on young elk and buffalo and fresh fish, but the festivities ended by sunset. It was time to lie down on a sweet bed of grass to think of the morrow and to sleep.

Another dawn came, and before orders were given to mount and march, a scouting patrol appeared from the northeast. They led a mare and a captive on foot. His outstretched arms were tied as he ran to keep up. Head down, he still ran with light feet. Minnetaka noted that he was about his age. A Chippewa.

It was soon learned that he had been captured in the hills southeast of Eagle Lake in a plum thicket. He was tied securely and made to squat in the center of the camp. All took time to look at close range into the face of the enemy. Many hurled insults, remembering the death and sorrow his people had brought upon the Dakotah, even though he was too young to have been party to past bloodshed.

A war council met to decide his fate. It was possible that other Chippewa scouts had seen and reported the Dakotah force. Very well, here was a messenger, and the message to the enemy would be simple – all Chippewa must leave the Kandiyohi Lakes, immediately. To demonstrate the violent history of tribal conflict, the young man would lose one finger. This was considered the least serious of penalties.

Minnetaka and Kiyi watched the sentence carried out. The Chippewa scout was ordered to step forward, now unbound, and place his right forefinger on a dry oak log. Two braves placed a knife-edged rock over the finger. Then another lifted a large stone and swung it down to strike exactly. The finger flipped off like a twig, but the scout showed no feeling of pain, only a tightening of his jaw. A glowing stick from a fire was applied to the stump at the knuckle to cauterize it and stop the bleeding, but the odor of burned flesh wafted about as if a reminder of future carnage.

Chief Grey Dog spoke: "We are sparing your life. Go back to your people. Tell them we are here and that tomorrow we will drive them out. If they listen to you, your message will save hundreds of your tribe."

He turned to the warriors who had carried out the punishment. "Strip him, tie his hands behind his back, and let him run the gauntlet as he leaves. That way he will remember upon whose lands he has trespassed."

At this announcement a roar went up. A double line was formed, everybody finding a willow switch.

"Minnetaka!" Kiyi yelled. "Here's a stick for you. Come on!"

But Minnetaka turned away, his mind again on the coming battle. Hundreds could die. Kitsey could easily be one of them. Here he was, a part of this force of hatred that could destroy her – and in doing so, destroy him.

"Wait!" It was Grey Dog who commanded. What now? There was a hush. "Where is Ghost Raven? Tell him to come forward. He knows the Chippewa language from his days east in Wisconsin."

The old chief spoke to Ghost Raven: "Tell the boy that there is still time to talk. Tell him that if his chief wants to save his people he will meet me on the highest hill that looks north across Medayto toward the Lower Falls. Tell him ..."

A murmur of protest had been growing until his voice could no longer be heard clearly. Some of the younger braves were showing their agitation. They wanted to fight. Nothing else would satisfy them.

Grey Dog's face was livid with anger. "Quiet! I am leader of this war party, and I will be heard! Yes, I want revenge ... but if we can have revenge without losing another Dakotah, then that is what I want!"

He waited until the clamor abated. "Tell the boy that his chief and other chiefs and medicine men must come in no more than four canoes. They must be on the water moving toward us at dawn. If not, the battle begins."

The young scout nodded and spoke rapidly to Ghost Raven who turned and interpreted: "He understands and will report what you have said. But ... he says, if you do attack it will be no easy victory for you. All of their camps have been alerted."

"Huh!" Grey Dog looked scornfully at the youth. "Tell him that we have no fear. One Dakotah warrior is worth five Chippewa!"

At his signal the youth was set free to run the gauntlet. He crouched low, taut, then bounded like a deer, dodging from side to side. His speed and agility made half the blows miss him, reminding many that the enemy was quick, brave and cunning.

After the evening meal was over, and fires dotted the entire island, the muffled beat of tom toms could be heard as drummers practiced their cadences. Teen-age boys began to dance, their supple, young bodies surrendering to the demanding rhythm. Others joined them, chanting in unison about heroes, gods and battles, as if to reassure themselves about the coming day.

Gathering of the Tribes

Minnetaka watched. Listening made his stomach quiver. The drums demanded response, and the only response was to dance. To dance meant to twirl and bounce with the beat. Agitated and excited, the warriors focused their wrath upon the enemy. To the chanting was added war whoops, one group calling, another group replying. Some were already in war paint; blotches of black, white, yellow and red completely disguised their identity. As they danced the perspiration streaked their makeup. He wanted to dance, but he felt too depressed, thinking of Kitsey. Yes, he thought, tomorrow the passion of the dance would be replaced by the passion of battle.

At dawn Kiyi awakened Minnetaka: "Quick, get up! We're ready to leave. The scouts are on their way. Here, I brought you some pemmican ... and I've packed enough for both of us to last two days."

They ate quickly, then joined the other warriors who were checking out their weapons, ponies and war paint. Eagle and other feathers and body paint made each man a fierce, artistic creation.

War paint was supplied by using various colored clays, charcoal and vegetable dyes. Red was from bits of iron found in clay hillsides. Orange and white came from decaying rocks. Soot and bear grease produced a shiny black. Pure yellow was rare, as was bright blue.

Minnetaka confronted Kiyi. "How do I look? I want to look like a warrior ... not a boy playing warrior."

"The black paint disguises your age. Your eyes encircled with white make you look frightening. How about me? I like red and black, and I made my mouth wide with white to make it look like I'll eat the enemy like a wolf! Today some enemy may see our faces as a last sight before going to their distant hunting ground."

The two friends had been assigned as runners along with several other young warriors. They fell in line behind the main party. The chiefs were mounted on the first and largest horses. Warriors of each tribe kept in a body, except for those already on the flanking movements. By moving in a fairly straight line toward Lake Medayto, they would arrive when the early sun was still caught in the highest tree branches. If the chief of the Chippewa had received the ultimatum, he would be nearing the south shore look-out about the same time.

Upon arrival at the south shore of Medayto the runners were instructed to bring dry wood for a signal fire, then green weeds and tree leaves. The huge pile was sprinkled with dry hay to make the smoke white and visible. As yet there were no signs of movement on the glittering lake. Grey Dog was angry and impatient.

"Do you see anybody?" he shouted. He stared, shading his eyes, but his sight was failing.

"Yes, yes!" someone answered. "I see canoes in the distance."

"How many?"

"Four canoes."

Chief Grey Dog sat down with a grunt. He nodded. "The enemy is wise. Let us hope. Above all, let us watch for trickery. But no .. if there are only four canoes, their chief cannot deceive us. He must know that there are several war parties moving in several directions ... that we are here in force."

Minnetaka and Kiyi and the other runners also squatted, awaiting orders. If there were to be a battle, their task, an important one, would begin. Their mission was to carry information back and forth to the main observation points. Once fighting started, progress was difficult to ascertain. Only the runners could provide current news that might mean the difference between victory and defeat.

While others grumbled, whetted knifes, drew bows in practice, paced, Minnetaka was silent. It seemed that only he could read the mind of Grey Dog whose head had fallen forward as if in meditation. They wanted the same thing – no battle. But for him, a hot-blooded young warrior, to betray such a thought, was treasonous. The chief, like Tya, knew that bloodshedding might never settle the differences forever between the Dakotah and Chippewa. Neither wanted more of their family to die unnecessarily.

The sun had risen fully. Minnetaka felt faint when he sat in the open, away from the great oak trees. Where was Kitsey at this moment? Did she think he had forsaken her. When they had parted that night of perfection and love, it had been quietly understood that what would happen would happen. It was the adult way to think; it was fate. Yet, he could not accept that they and their youth might be wasted.

"Are you all right?" Kiyi asked.

"Sure." He grinned and punched his friend in the chest. "I'm ready to eat a wild cat instead of pemmican!"

Despite his outward show of bravado, his inner voice kept saying: Kitsey, Kitsey, where are you?

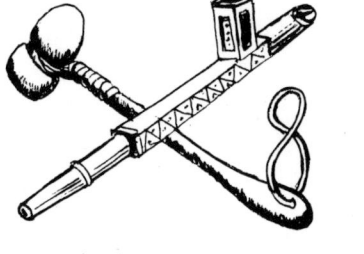

17
Negotiation

Kitsey had awakened to abnormal activity in the main camp. The old squaws were quarrelsome. She was given orders to help with the packing. Even the children were hushed, noticing that something was amiss. The men had vanished. She asked the old squaw who had befriended her what was wrong.

"Dakotah! Your people!" She spat on the ground at Kitsey's feet. "Now get busy before I beat you!"

She joined in the assembling of foods, clothing, utensils, only those items that were portable. As she tied a bundle, two warriors approached from nowhere. She was bewildered. They told her to hold out her hands. She was bound and led away toward the shore and commanded to get into a large canoe, one of four being readied for launching. She knew now that whatever was happening was of the gravest importance. Undoubtedly, the Dakotah Nation had come north to make war, as she and Minnetaka had expected.

She pondered her role, but knew all she could do was to remain silent.

In the first canoe she recognized Chief Iron Hand. From the old squaw she had learned that he was a great leader in war, but also a man who desired peace. His wise council was much sought after even in matters as small as domestic quarrels. Born near Kathio on Lake Millacs, he was the son of Chief Cyunna who had led his people against the Dakotah in a decisive battle which had given them the northern lakes.

The flotilla of canoes approached the high bank on the south shore. An intimidating column of smoke rose skyward. The four large canoes were beached at the rocky point. The chiefs climbed a path that led up to the grassy meadow.

Council of War — South Shore of Medayto

Kitsey was unbound and Iron Hand came to her and said, "You speak the Dakotah language. Tell the Dakotah chiefs that we come in peace, to talk. Tell them also that my warriors and chiefs will not, under any circumstances, be threatened, insulted or harmed. She nodded.

As a young woman she had never anticipated being chosen for such an important duty. True, she had re-learned the Chippewa language, but it was not a female's place to be the main interpreter between two nations. Nevertheless, she felt confident and, in a clear, strong voice, she greeted the already assembled Dakotah war party, repeating Iron Hand's words.

Chief Grey Dog had risen, erect and alert. "Tell Iron Hand we honor him. As one we all join in our promise of peaceful consultation. Be seated."

It was apparent to all that Iron Hand commanded great respect from his own men. He also had an air about him that drew respect from those seeing him for the first time. He was an imposing figure, not as old as Grey Dog, with the broad shoulders of a wrestler. His wide face was cheerful, his features almost boyish, his black eyes glistening and alert as if a window into his mind. And for a chief, he was simply dressed: laced buckskin leggings, a buckskin tunic, unadorned, elkhide moccasins, a wide, beaded headband and a necklace.

Iron Hand, Chief of the Chippewas

"Iron Hand," Grey Dog said, arms folded, "You and your warriors are our guests. We meet today on a most important matter."

Kitsey interpreted.

Grey Dog continued: "We the Dakotah are a mighty nation. Our brothers are scattered across the prairies as far as five days journey from this place. They have come in force to reclaim their ancestral lands, the Kandiyohi Lakes. The food we need is in these lakes."

Kitsey repeated each word in her head and then spoke slowly.

The old chief continued. "Blood has been drawn on many occasions in the past. Women and children have been killed. Camps and food supplies have been destroyed. It is time for this to stop. Representing the seven Dakotah Tribes, I, Chief Grey Dog, ask you to return to your traditional homeland to the north, in peace. Chief Iron Hand, hear my words. I have spoken."

Kitsey repeated. All eyes were on her. All waited for her to become confused. Her sentences were short and direct, taking one chief's thoughts and conveying them to the other.

It was Iron Hand's turn to speak: "Chief Grey Dog, we too come in peace. Certainly we all can feel the Great Spirit as it sends this warm sun. The earth mother is bountiful. There are lakes, fish and game for all. Let us not be jealous. Let us rather be generous.

"But we have problems today." He had been smiling, but now his eyes flashed, and he continued with a frown. "We had problems long ago. Our people were driven out of Michigan. We had to expand west for more food. And so you, like us, were driven west to Wisconsin and Minnesota.

"Many, many moons ago our tribes clashed in the huge battle of Kathio. After several days and hundreds killed and wounded, our people separated to their present homelands. We remained to the north, you in the south. these lakes in between are claimed by both. We are here today to settle this difference.

"The Chippewa are not afraid to die. We have reports on your numbers from our scouts. One Finger Left Behind also reported on your camp at the Victor's Island." He was almost smiling as he went on. "My warriors are ready. Our campfires ring the lake. Hunting parties from our many camps are now back at Medayto. We can match your numbers."

Iron Hand was now walking back and forth, his words coming faster. Kitsey found herself repeating his words with some emotion. This was noticed by all. None approved. Iron Hand stopped. Now he was looking skyward. He went on. "Guarantee us our safe passage back to our camp at the Lower Falls. Then attack any time you are ready. My men have been ready since daylight."

Chief Grey Dog said, "Very well, Iron Hand, you have spoken. We have heard you, and you have said nothing new. Yes, we both claim these lakes, but you forget that we claimed them long before your people descended from the north. Your safe return is assured ... but hear Chief Long Walk of the Sissetons before you depart."

Chief Long Walk was a tall warrior in full war paint. His lean features had a fierce, menacing appearance. He had been a leader of many war parties. His bravery in battle was subject of many story-telling sessions around the campfires. He approached Iron Hand, leaving Kitsey between them.

"Chief Iron Hand, we too know your strength. Your warriors are brave, but it will be a one-sided battle. Our numbers are again as many as yours. Watch the hills. They are alive with Dakotahs from many distant places."

At a nod from Chief Grey Dog the pyre of grass and sticks was set ablaze. A column of white smoke rose high in the still air.

Long Walk continued. "Now look to the east. Soon you will see our signal in smoke between Eagle and Manah Lakes. Our men there are alerted and ready to attack. Likewise, look to the high point overlooking Eagle Lake ... west to the High Lakes, and farther west to the Four Lakes ... yes, and north to Mount Toma. There are the Wahpetons, the Poncas, the Sissetons, the Ogalalas, the Winnebagoes, and the Wanamingos ... in the hundreds!"

Kitsey begged him to slow down, but he ignored her and walked away.

Old Chief Grey Dog came forth again. "The warm sun is in the sky, Chief Iron Hand. The day is young. Counsel your warriors to retreat to Kathio. Take your wigwams, your canoes, your women, your children, before it is too late. It takes bravery to wage war, but it takes bravery to make peace also."

Kitsey had become the voice link between the two factions. Her conveyance of words was at times automatic. She was at times searching with her eyes in the wide circle for a familiar figure, but in war paint individual identity was lost. Grey Dog asked if she wanted water. She nodded.

"Water ... water for the girl."

Out jumped a volunteer, Kiyi. As he passed her the water jar he whispered, "I am Minnetaka's friend."

She glanced about. "Where is he?"

He took the water from her. "Coming," he said.

Iron Hand began to speak again, diverting her attention. "I do indeed seek peace ... but my warriors seek blood. Their memories are fresh from past battles. So, we leave now. At the end of this day we will know who owns the Kandiyohi Lakes. May the Great Spirit help us all."

There was tension in the air. It emanated from each individual. But the tension of negotiation was replaced with thoughts of conflict, suffering and death. Peaceful exchange was being replaced by a deeply concealed savagery. The drums began a slow, mournful beat. It seemed to predict both the violence of combat and the sorrow of dead and dying.

The Chippewa with quiet dignity returned to their large canoes. Their paddles flashed in unison in the bright morning sun as their steady chant was carried back by a gentle breeze. The chance for peace, now lost, was symbolized by the flotilla as it became smaller on the huge lake.

The huge fire was lit, its black smoke towering skyward. To the south, to the east and to the west fires answered. The battle had begun.

Kitsey had searched the crowd of painted faces in vain for Minnetaka. He had to be nearby, but where? Once on the narrow strip of white sand beach, she had given up hope. Small waves sifted and packed firm a narrow band of wet sand at her feet. In the water were a variety of colored stones, and clamshells catching in the sunlight. How cruel to be reminded.

Suddenly she had heard a voice speaking her name clearly. She turned to face Minnetaka in his fierce mask. She would not have been able to recognize him.

Her captors had been impatient. She could sense their irritation over the delay of the last canoe.

Minnetaka had turned his back on her when he whispered, "Wait ... I'll come." Then he left abruptly.

Wait? Where? When? Did he consider that she was still a prisoner, that a battle was to begin? Who could predict the winner or the loser? Individuals caught up in it were as leaves tossed by the wind. "Wait, I'll come," did not offer comfort. It did speak of Minnetaka's love and concern. That was all she had as she was pushed toward the canoe. She had to have faith. He said he would come. Yes, he would come.

The old chief, Grey Dog, confronted his assembly of Dakotah leaders after the departure of the Chippewa. There were murmurs of hostility. He understood. He had given the hated enemy safe passage out of the area without bloodshed, receiving nothing in return. He had been willing to call off the encounter his tribal brothers had traveled so far to take part in.

He ignored their grumbling. They wanted to spill blood, but it was he who must lead after the battle. The continuation of the tribe was his responsibility. It included women and children who might become widows and orphans. With more than four hundred men at his command, his thoughts were on saving lives. It would call upon all his knowledge and experience to carry out the strategy that would defeat the enemy without unnecessary losses.

"We are here to do battle," he announced. "There is no longer a choice. The signal fires are lit, the other tribes are attacking the outlying camps." He raised his arms high. "Remember, the Chippewa are at home in the Big Woods. You will feel their arrows before you hear them. They know the art of camouflage. Bush, swamp grass, hide them. If a group suddenly retreats and launches canoes, do not be tempted. Suddenly you will be trapped farther up the shore, and you will become like geese without wings. Take no prisoners! Now, attack!"

Minnetaka shuddered. What hope was there for Kitsey?

The chiefs and warriors, now released, again called up their hatred to rekindle their courage. With animal yells they mounted milling ponies ... ponies which they would have to leave behind once they got to the Big Woods. Spears, tomahawks, battle ensigna were thrust skyward as each group rode off, all of them convinced they were unconquerable.

18
The Battle

Minnetaka and Kiyi had been given the assignment to ride in the open country to the west and report any concentration or movement of the enemy. The narrow strips of land between the High Lakes and the Twin Lakes were portages to be watched.

In a short time they reached warriors from the Wahpeton and Sisseton Tribes who were on the offensive, searching the wooded hills. Scouts reported good progress and little resistance in the area.

After that, the two were to continue on to the Big Woods where every man might be needed. With reluctance, they tied their horses in some dense cedars by the High Lakes. The day was bright and warm, the sky blue, the lakes sparkling. There seemed to be no war, no enemy, no cause for fear. But they knew otherwise. From now on a crunch of a twig underfoot could be fatal.

Each had a bow and about thirty arrows. Each had a war club made of a stone laced to a white ash handle. Both had flint knives, much like long spear heads. Each weapon demanded all the users' skill and strength.

They had been told by the elders that the effectiveness of these weapons depended on deep hate, that in hand-to-hand combat you became as an animal. Your actions became purely instinctive. Your attacker wanted you dead by fair means or foul. There were no concessions to your youth, your experience or lack of it. Your opponent might have much in his favor, such as numbers, concealment, knowledge of terrain.

As they set out on foot, Kiyi said, "I expect to come back, don't you?"

"If we have courage, we'll have the help of the Great Spirit. Then we'll come back."

They broke into a rhythmic, crouching trot, stopping occasionally to see where they were. The trees were becoming more dense.

THE BATTLE GROUND

CROW RIVER   (KARISHON)

NEST LAKE

THE BIG WOODS

GREEN LAKE (MEDAYTO)

GEORGE AND HENDERSON (HIGH LAKES)

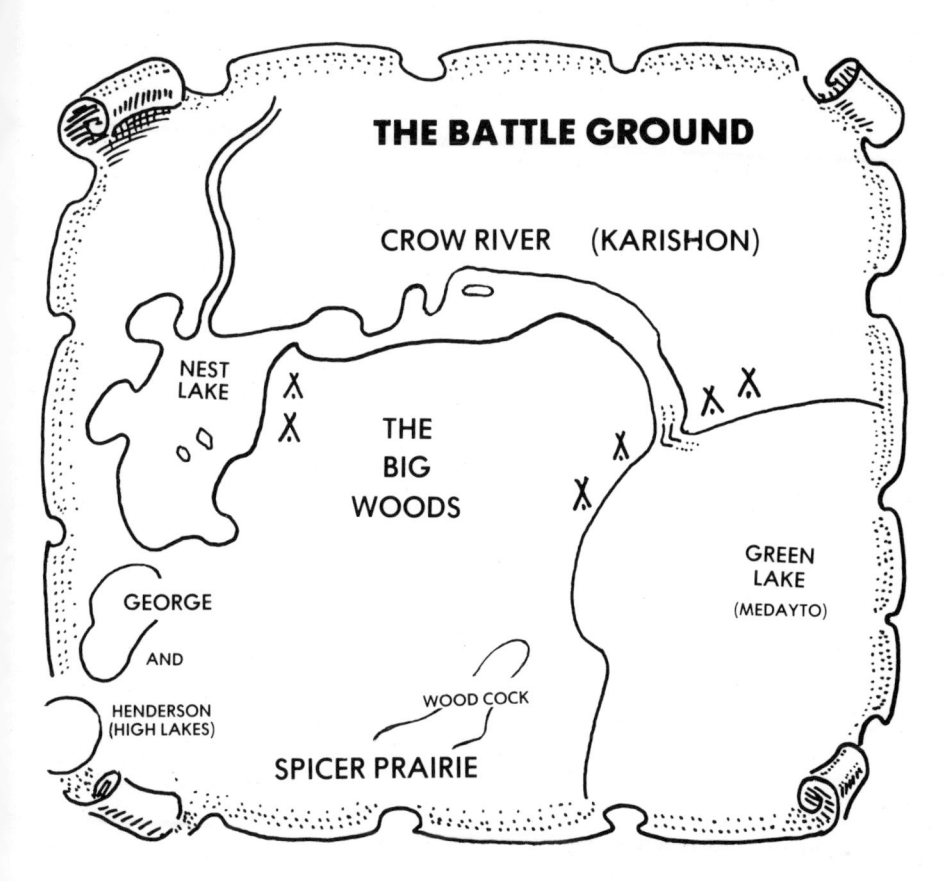

WOOD COCK

SPICER PRAIRIE

"Remember the chief's warnings," Minnetaka whispered. "The Chippewa are clever. They can be anywhere, above, below, in a crotch of a tree, behind a log covered with vines. Don't be tempted to follow anybody into swamp grass." He paused. "Kiyi, if I don't return from this battle you must speak on my behalf. I want my name to be worthy of my dead father and mother. My good friend, will you speak for me?"

I will speak for you, my friend ... if you die in battle."

"Let's go on," Minnetaka said. "We must have our ears alert and our eyes in the back."

To the trained eye there were trails leading around ponds and meadows which animals used. Hunters found them and traveled them, and so did Kiyi and Minnetaka, preferring them because they were free from twigs and overhanging shrubs.

Ahead was the south shore of Nest Lake. They were nearing the main battle and expected to hear something soon.

Suddenly Kiyi stopped. "Look, Minnetaka! Here, over here! Blood, it's blood!"

"Quiet! Move slowly. Be ready. Whether the enemy numbers two or ten we are alone. We live and die together."

It was fresh blood, no doubt about it. They heard a noise, a groan, but nothing was visible. Then a slight movement in the grass exposed an arrow, its feathered shaft pointing upward. It was a wounded man. They approached cautiously. It could be an ambush. The man tried to sit up, groaning.

Certain that he was helpless, they came up to him. Blood was running from a scalp wound, mixing with dirt and war paint which covered most of his face. Two arrows protruded from his stomach ... Dakotah arrows. He seemed not to notice them. It was clear that he was dying.

The two friends looked at each other. What to do with him? There was no conflict, no victory. Yet, he was the enemy. He may have killed one of their own this very day. A quick, sudden death was the solution. As warriors they must hurry on.

"Pull his loin cloth over his face. We'll each hit his head," Minnetaka said.

The force of their blows echoed like hitting a hollow log. The man's body stiffened, then relaxed as blood gushed from his nose and mouth. A scalp held no glory.

In silence they pushed on through the woods, coming upon a deserted Chippewa camp. Fires still smoked, but all was quiet. They were at the east shore of Nest Lake now and the paths were well-worn, ahead was the place opposite where Minnetaka had waited in his cave for Kitsey.

They heard sounds of battle. Kiyi chose to run, and soon Minnetaka was matching him stride for stride, both eager to take part in the main action.

Although they knew the battle plan, they could not know how cautiously Chief Grey Dog's primary drive from the Medayto Prairie had begun. The chief was mindful of the many Chippewas fighting in an area so well-known to them. A dead warrior could not fight; staying alive was each individual's responsibility. In an area where visibility was poor it was safer to move in groups of four or five with one man leading. Upon sighting an enemy, or being attacked, the lead man would fall back rather than fight one to one. Each tribe, in fact, understood that it was better to have a four or five to one advantage. Heroes had short lives. Patience and stealth were the fine points that ensured a victory.

Still running, but slower, along a path close to the bank of the river, they made their way toward the battle sounds. Suddenly Kiyi screamed, "I'm hit, Minnetaka!" Minnetaka stopped and saw an arrow in Kiyi's lower back, almost under the arm. He turned, looking for the enemy bowman, but saw no one. He must be below the bank. There might be more than one. They were targets now.

"Go back," Minnetaka said. "Hide below the trail, keep out of sight. I'll return soon."

He waited until Kiyi stumbled in retreat, blood running down his side. Minnetaka crouched low and ran towards a tree near the riverbank. From there he had protection from below. There was a sound, a splash. The assailant had decided to try to swim out of range.

Throwing aside his weapons, except for his tomahawk and knife, Minnetaka slid down the bank and dove into the river. At midstream he overtook the Chippewa warrior who swam with one hand, the other holding his bow. Hearing his swift pursuer, he was not looking back.

In a few powerful strokes Minnetaka had caught up with the glistening, black head. He took the tomahawk out of his waistband and with one wild growl he drove the enemy head underwater with a crushing blow. Blood streamed in the current. Minnetaka grabbed the floating, bloody hair. With his flint knife, he made a long cut above the eyebrows, and slashed to the sides, feeling the skin come free from the bone. Peeling it back as the body floated downstream, he ripped it away, his first scalp. The body turned in the current, the face became visible. It was the face of a youth who had paid for a foolish act which he mistook for bravery.

Back ashore, Minnetaka found Kiyi panting, hidden under some brush. He was conscious and not bleeding heavily. The arrow had entered the right lower back at an angle that would have allowed it to pass through flesh and perhaps come out clean. Instead, it had glanced off a rib and the shaft was broken. The head of the arrow lay deep in flesh.

"Kiyi, I can pull it out if you can stand the pain."

"Pull it out," Kiyi groaned.

Minnetaka grabbed the broken arrow. Putting his foot along side of it, he pulled upward. Kiyi grunted, but the worst was yet to come. Minnetaka adjusted his angle, braced himself and yanked again. This time the arrow came out. Stuffing the hole with a hollow reed for drainage, and cattail down for sponge, the bleeding was soon under control. But Kiyi lay heaving from tension and pain.

Minnetaka tried to conceal his impatience, it was rooted in his concern for Kitsey. He wanted to run ahead to join the encirclement at the Lower Falls, but Kiyi was his friend, his responsibility.

Sensing his eagerness, Kiyi sat up. "I'm not bleeding. I can walk now."

"Are you sure. Do you feel your strength coming back? You will need it. We must be ready if attacked."

Kiyi got up, painfully, nodding.

As they continued along the path, the cries of battle seemed to diminish. Looking far up river they saw canoes moving swiftly downstream.

"Look, Minnetaka, eight canoes! Let's try to catch up with them."

As they watched, the canoes swept into the opposite shore and picked up Chippewa warriors, then sped onward downstream towards the Falls and Medayto.

"There's nothing we can do," Minnetaka said. "But our war party will soon be at the main camp to intercept them."

He started to run, then slowed down until Kiyi caught up, eager to get to the Chippewa's main camp. Kitsey, Kitsey, was all he could think. When they approached the Falls they heard little sound of battle. The camp was abandoned.

Before the battle was to begin, Chief Grey Dog called the chiefs together. "Brothers today we are warriors. Your life, my life could end this day. Hear me as I review our plan of battle. Remember, we play into the enemy hand by being caught in any high concentration. This leads to close hand-to-hand fighting with many casualties on both sides. Order your warriors to move in groups of five, moving forward, but also laterally if terrain requires it. When resistance is encountered fall back and wait for the enemy to expose his positions. Then attack when you have support. Tell your men to be patient. Time is on our side. Our numbers will assure the victory."

With those words Grey Dog gave a yell like a dog - a dog howl at night. A chorus of war cries followed, starting with the chiefs and spreading to each warrior. It was a chilling, convincing act of hate, revenge, and inner discipline. It was a challenge hurled at death. It was the combined power of the Sioux nation.

The Sioux, leaving their horses behind, were on foot in a heavily timbered area called the Big Woods. It was boxed in by Nest Lake on the west. The Karishon across the north side and Medayto making up the east border. The south boundary was the wide open Medayto Prairie.

This confined space of four or five square miles granted the superior force many advantages. Most important was the relatively small size of the area. This would tend to intensify, but shorten the battle. Secondly, the enemy being driven by a force from the south had no option when retreat was necessary. Thirdly, the open waterways gave overall visibility in the instance where reinforcements were being brought in, or in a retreat involving use of canoes.

The disadvantage was the poor visibility. This would be a problem for each warrior. It would also reduce the ability of the leaders to evaluate the tide of the battle.

Minnetaka and Kiyi had seen or heard little of the battle. The encounter with the wounded Chippewa and the young warrior told them that the enemy had moved south to intercept the Sioux. There was no way of knowing if they were part of a large group that was sent to confront the Sioux en-mass.

They had heard yells when the wind died down, but they were far away and could not be distinguished as to whether they were friend or foe. If all was going according to plan there should be a gradual movement by the Sioux in a northerly direction. They were to learn later that the hottest battle took place near Woodcock Lake. The east edge of Woodcock is but a few hundred yards from Medayto. On the west end of Woodcock it is about a mile to Nest Lake. There are smaller ponds and marshes in the same area.

The main forces clashed in these strategic areas. The Chippewas fought bravely and with great effectiveness until the superior numbers of the Sioux were brought to bear.

Once having gained an advantage, the Sioux took time to group their forces and plan an orderly movement to drive the Chippewas to the river. This delay, while good strategy, was to give the Chippewas the opportunity to carry out a plan that had been in the mind of Iron Hand since his scouts had come back with reports of a heavy concentration of Sioux.

19
Chippewa Deception

"Minnetaka, the battle is over! The Chippewas never planned a full fledged confrontation." Kiyi was clearly disappointed. He laughed and moaned at the same time. "We've driven them out from the lakes, Minnetaka. They fled like rabbits!"

Minnetaka knew better. He walked to the Lower Falls, and saw the departing Chippewa canoes, the last ones, glistening paddles in the noonday sun. Nobody had stopped them. The Dakotahs had pursued others up the shoreline, into the vast woods, against Chief Grey Dog's orders. The Chippewas had not been defeated; they had just withdrawn, only to return some day. Minnetaka knew that. Grey Dog knew that. Tya knew that.

And where was Kitsey? He sat down, dejected.

Yes, it is over, he thought – for another season. This time they had prevailed, but without a real victory. The Kandiyohi Lakes would continue, as they had for many moons, to be the prize to be sought by succeeding generations.

There was disappointment in the Dakotah Camp that afternoon at the Lower Falls, as they took possession of the empty wigwams. No food had been left behind, no weapons, only smoking embers of fires. True, fifty or more of the enemy had been killed. Twenty-two Dakotah warriors lay dead, and as many more were wounded.

Iron Hand had escaped with hundreds of his people to the east, across Lake Medayto, into Loon Lake and from there to the safety of the Karishon River flowing east. Not a woman, not a child, had been slain or left behind. The victory for the Sioux was an empty one.

However, in a few hours Dakotah women arrived with pack horses and an abundance of food. Fires had been rekindled, some teepees were put up in preference to the hated enemy dwellings.

The pent-up emotions soon turned to talking and laughing as the Dakotahs realized that they had reclaimed their lakes. After the Minnesota Prairie the beauty of the Medayto was impressive. Cool swims, excellent fish catches, abundant game in the woods, did away with the tensions.

But Minnetaka could not share in the jubilance. Kitsey was somewhere waiting, he was sure of that. She had promised to wait, but where?

There was to be a victory celebration, even though it was tarnished by the cunning of Iron Hand. It was important to all who took part and survived, but for some it would be measured with the loss of a husband, a son, a close friend. Light as the losses were, it could not be forgotten that men had died, women were made widows, and some children were made orphans. The tribes would have fewer hunters, but more mouths to feed next winter.

Kiyi was recovering well. Minnetaka had told him of his plans to leave in search of Kitsey.

"Do you have much pain?" Minnetaka asked.

"Not much, now. I can ride."

"I'm going to leave, if you are all right."

"I'm all right."

"Then I'll go."

"Kiyi" exclaimed Minnetaka, "Kitsey is gone. Did she stay with the retreating Chippewas? Did she choose to go with them or was she forced to go with them? She promised to wait for me, but I don't know where she might be. She could be a captive, she could be killed, if the Chippewas decided she was valuable to the Sioux if allowed to return."

Minnetaka continued, "I'm hoping she escaped before the battle. I hope she is hiding and waiting somewhere. I'm going along the north shore of Medayto. I want to go alone. Time is of no importance. I won't be back until I am again with her. Tell Tya."

"Minnetaka ... the Chippewas have scattered. Who knows where Kitsey might be? Where would you look? You will be alone in Chippewa country. You don't know the country. Think carefully. It could be your very life. I too want to see Kitsey, but I want to see you together, alive. Go, my friend, if you must. May the Great Spirit protect you. I will listen to your signal of the little owl after sundown."

"Will you take Blackie to Red Wood for me?"

"Of course, we may start our return at daylight."

As he walked away, Minnetaka felt empty. The battle and the victory were not up to his expectations. Where was the glory? Even the killing of two Chippewas seemed a needless act. They were humans, young men like himself. There was plenty of space and food for their existence. Had Iron Hand chosen to stay in the northern lakes, they would still be alive.

Kiyi had been a casualty; he was now a seasoned warrior, wounded in battle. But, being shot from ambush by an arrow was not glory, not a story to be told around campfires. Minnetaka's retaliation, proved by the scalp on his belt, had received enthusiastic approval, but he did not feel like boasting about it.

Tya would say that he had avenged two of her loved ones. Good. He wanted to do that much for her, for her chopped-off fingers.

But, he still felt empty.

He would never feel otherwise until he found Kitsey.

20
Cass-Teo

To find Kitsey, Minnetaka sensed that he must walk east along the north shore. He would cross at the Lower Falls where young boys were spearing buffalo fish and northern pike. The tribes of the Wanamingoes and the Winnebagoes were camped along the east side of the Falls as well as farther east along the lake, wherever a level site was available.

He walked among their teepees, hugging the shore where the lake banks were low and following well worn paths that by-passed the high wooded knolls which fronted to the south, overlooking the lake.

Soon the teepees were behind him and he was alone in the early evening. There was tension in both his mind and body. It reminded him of his running on the bluffs of the big valley he called his home.

He allowed his mind to think of Tya. She had reminded him that his life was important and that war would not bring peace. The battle results would have pleased her. She would rather be tricked by the enemy than to have lost half the Sioux warriors in an evenly fought blood bath. The vague pain he felt was that of a lonely child. He would be happy to be back with her.

Presently he came to a long narrow low-lying beach which separated the lake from a large shallow swamp. The white sand at water's edge made a firm footing. It was an invitation to run.

As he ran an occasional frog awaited his approach before hurling himself into the shallow riffles. Beyond the first riffles there was a band of pebbles of various colors. Among them were clam shells rubbed pearly white by heavy wave action. Why hadn't he been looking for a sign from Kitsey? He must be looking for clam shells in a pattern that was conspicuous to his eyes alone. Could he have missed her signs? He looked ahead along the sandy beach. Was his eyesight unreliable in this half light?

There seemed to be an animal drinking from the lake. Presently it moved back out of sight. It could be a deer. It could be a wolf or small bear. It could also be a human - an enemy. It could be several of the enemy. Whatever it was, it didn't seem alarmed.

Minnetaka instinctively sought the shelter of the willows and pin oaks that covered the sandy bank. He sought the game trail that paralleled the shore. Proceeding cautiously, he tuned his ears to pick up every sound. His trained ear ignored the sounds near at hand and focused towards the image he had seen ahead. At interludes he would stop, hoping to hear or see something. The loud wail and wistful reply of two loons relieved his tension. If they were not alarmed, perhaps he had little to fear.

He had decided that whatever it was it was more likely to be animal than man. Relieved he again chose the beach for walking. The still evening welcomed a half moon in the eastern sky. Suddenly his eyes were drawn downward. There on the wet sand lay three shells. Two were close together. All were in a line. It was as if the single clam was directing the way. There was no mistake this was Kitsey's sign, but where was she?

He looked about holding his breath to better hear. Now a light mist was lifting over the large swamp beyond the sand bank. The combination of moonlight and mist made images dance in eyes that were straining for a sign of the one person who could bring sunshine into his life. He walked on and hesitated again. At a distance he heard the soft hoot of the tiny screech owl. While he listened the call was repeated. It was still very soft. He turned in the direction of the call. Now it was repeated very clearly, very near at hand. Then out from behind a small thicket stepped Kitsey. As she approached him he was soon able to see the amused smile on her face. "To see you alive and well is the answer to all my prayers," whispered Kitsey.

"The Great Spirit sees us, his children and keeps us from harm. Kitsey, your life is my richest treasure," Minnetaka replied.

She confronted him and passed her arms around him with the flat of her hand high on his shoulders. She drew him close and pillowed her head on his bare chest. "Minnetaka, tell me now, and tell me that I am forever yours."

Minnetaka, bending forward, had enfolded her in his long arms. "We are one, but with two beating hearts. I can feel the pulsating of your heart. It beats for me. Against your ear you hear my heart, it beats for you." Taking a deep breath they lost themselves in a kissing ritual of commitment.

"I know a high bank that overlooks the lake. It is just beyond us. It is near the point called Lone Tree. It will be an ideal place to spend the night," said Minnetaka.

On the knoll there were signs that it had often been used for council fires. It was flat and covered with knee high grass. The bank down to the lake was steep. The water lapping the stones below made a pleasant sound. Far in the distance to the west fires still burned in the Sioux camp. To the east was the outlet into the Karishon River. It was the route taken by the retreating Chippewas.

Lovers

By scraping a shallow bowl out of the soft earth, Minnetaka built a small almost concealed fire. It gave light to their young faces, especially their flashing eyes lit with a shared sense of delightful adventure.

There was so much to talk about. They had the whole night to talk.

"How were you captured at Four Lakes?" asked Minnetaka. "When did you become aware of my hiding in the cave? How were you treated as a captive?"

Kitsey replied, "I walked a short way from the Four Lakes Camp and into the hands of two Chippewas who had watched our camp for five days. They were sent to bring me back. It was all so easily done."

Minnetaka asked, "Why did they want you back?"

Kitsey replied, "Remember I was born a Chippewa. It would reflect on the honor of the tribe to allow the Sioux to keep a Chippewa against her will."

Minnetaka, "But you were brought up as a Sioux. Did you want to become a Chippewa again?"

Kitsey, "No. I know nothing of Chippewa ways."

Stretched out, facing the lake, with their shoulders touching they shared the little fire ahead of them. It wasn't that the summer evening was cool, but the fire reflected the light and warmth that the young people felt for each other.

Minnetaka continued, "Were you treated well at the Chippewa Camp?"

Kitsey, "I was watched. I was threatened. I expected that a battle was being planned. But most of all I sensed that you would find a way of freeing me. I had no idea of escape without help. I often imagined that you and Blackie would pick me up and we would outrun all the pursuers."

Minnetaka, "Did the squaws treat you well?"

Kitsey, "I belonged to four squaws. They were all wives of an old chief.

The oldest one had the most authority. She treated me well. Sometimes she would protect me from the others."

Minnetaka, "Do you mean other squaws?"

Kitsey, "Other squaws and also some older men."

Minnetaka, "Tell me about the men."

Kitsey, "I'd rather that you tell me about your experiences in battle. Was Kiyi with you?"

Minnetaka, "Kiyi and I were together. Kiyi was wounded by an arrow. The Chippewa paid with his life. I have the scalp buried in an ant hill."

Kitsey, "Why an ant hill?"

Minnetaka, "The ants eat away all meat and fat, leaving only the skin and hair. It is better than scraping."

Kitsey, "Chief Iron Hand gave the order for all women and children to go by boat at night. I was held back. I didn't dare to imagine the reason why. It turned out that he needed me as an interpreter. It gave me a chance to see you. You told me to wait. I waited here. And now we are here together." Kitsey parted his hanging hair to see him better. Leaning towards him she turned his face towards her and with a new aggression gave him a lingering kiss.

The moon had climbed higher. The breeze increased. An occasional mosquito insisted on gaining attention. As the fire burned low the couple sought warmth in the contact of their nude bodies.

Their cautious experiments led to a natural response. Their young bodies alternately resisting and inviting roused in each of them a feeling so new, so powerful and so exquisitely delightful that there seemed no place to stop. Drained of all energy they rolled over to look skyward. Still holding hands they soon were asleep.

As the moon moved into the western sky dawn was lighting the eastern horizon. The young lovers now huddled together for warmth found each other compatible again. Dosing; half awake, half asleep they awaited daylight.

Cass-Teo

Their personal passionate interlude was soon broken. Kitsey whispered, "Minnetaka, I see an animal." Minnetaka sat up, turning to Kitsey - questioning her whisper. At that moment a hideous scream was heard, as a huge body bounded towards them. It was Cass-Teo, a Chippewa renegade known for his crafty ways.

Cass-Teo dropped his knee in Minnetaka's stomach. Minnetaka groaned. He looked up into the fierce face and saw a tomahawk raised ready to break his skull. His upraised arm deflected some of the force, but a bloody gash on the head dulled his senses.

Kitsey, fearing for her life, grabbed Minnetaka's war club and from her knees swung with all her might. Her blow stunned Cass-Teo. Cass-Teo now crouched, lifted one leg and kicked outward into Kitsey's stomach, sending her into the nearby brush.

Minnetaka fought back dizziness. Without a war club he was defenseless. His serrated flint knife lay on the ground. Cass-Teo had not seen it. He noticed that Cass-Teo was moving slow. He decided to gamble. He would hurl himself at Cass-Teo's waist and drive him down the embankment. He had underestimated his huge opponent. A hard fist numbed his senses. As he slowly regained consciousness he was aware of a nauseating throbbing in his skull, steady dripping blood over his face, and his hands and feet tied with leather thongs. With the odds against him he had bravely gambled - and lost.

Cass-Teo had come for two captives. Once he had their feet tied he would be the captor. He quickly bound Minnetaka, both hand and foot.

Kitsey meanwhile thought of running, but with Minnetaka injured he needed help. Sensing further resistance was futile, especially with Cass-Teo's reputation, she rushed to Minnetaka's side shielding him from further attack.

The captives were tied hands behind their backs and around the ankles with enough leather rope to allow a short step.

Karishon at Medayto Outlet

Cass-Teo was a man of action. He led his captives down the shore to the outlet to the east. From a stand of thick cattails he produced a canoe. Before boarding the canoes he tied the ankles of the captives tight together. They were then lashed to the canoe. They understood. If the canoe was tipped they would very likely drown.

Cass-Teo hadn't explained what plans he had for his captives, but Kitsey knew all too well. Of the men in the Chippewa camp who kept watching her, Cass-Teo was the most feared.

His intentions were soon made clear. He would leave the Kandiyohi Lakes by way of the Karishon River.

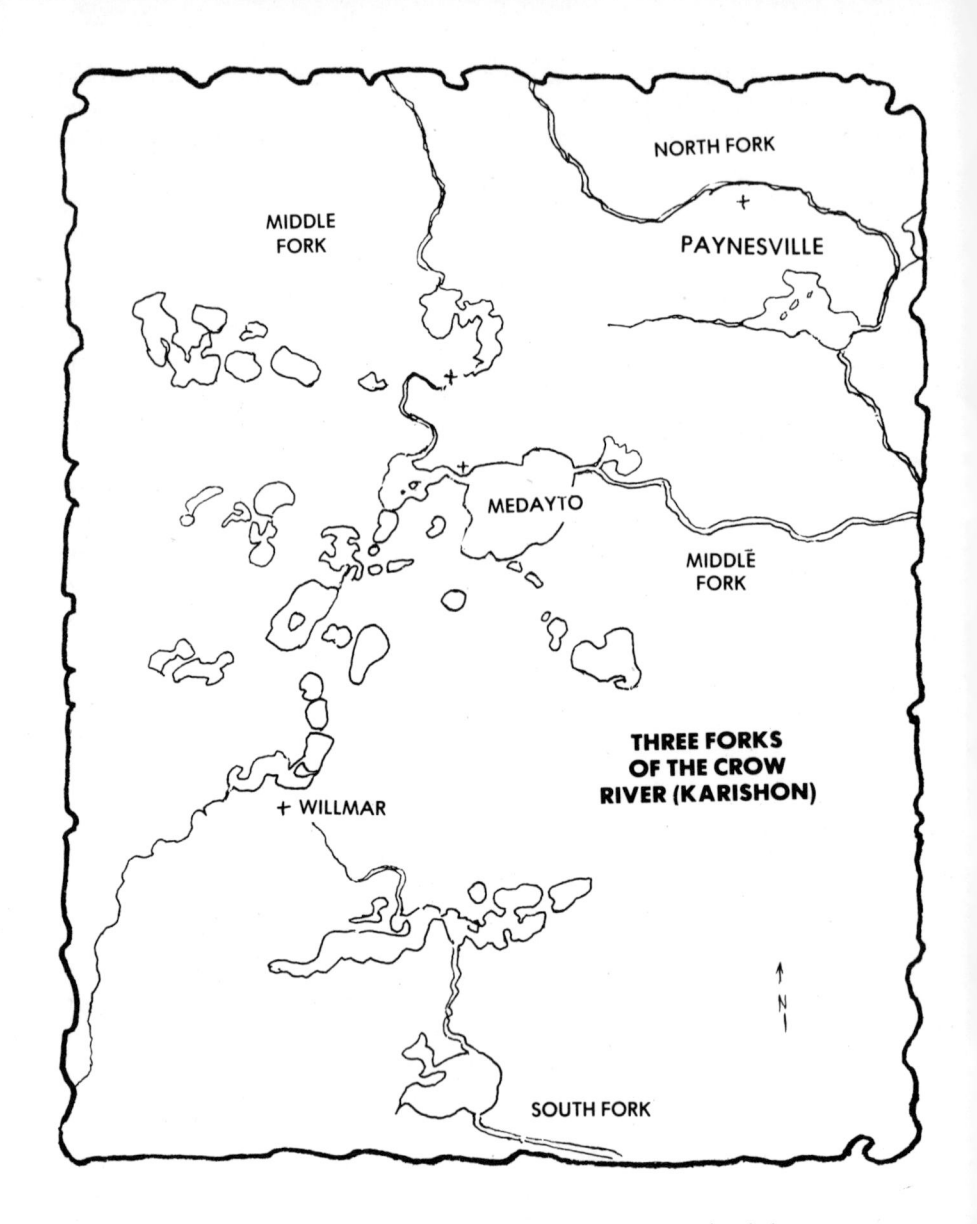

This free flowing stream has its source north of the New London Lakes. At New London, a water falls and rapids drop sixteen feet before continuing on to Nest Lake. It continues through Green Lake and flows east from the outlet towards villages; Manannah, Forest City, Rockford, Hanover and finally the Mississippi at Dayton.

The river running full made paddling almost unnecessary. It involved steering around windfalls and sharp bends in low areas. The trio moved faster than a man could walk. In three days they would be at the Father of Waters, the Mississippi.

Cass-Teo was a schemer, his own people mistrusted him. His actions were based on selfishness. Invariably he operated alone. Stealing from the enemy and bartering with his own people gave him a questionable reputation. That prevented old chiefs from giving him chief status. He was, everyone acknowledged, an excellent hunter. In battle he always survived. His broad frame and fierce facial features made him a person to remember. He made extra efforts to win the friendship of chiefs as he traveled alone from village to village. Today he had a cargo in great demand. The old chiefs would be interested.

Kitsey, would not be surprised. He had tormented her while she worked. Only the older squaw would send him away.

Cass-Teo had watched Kitsey since she was captured at Four Lakes months ago. He was not alone. The teenage braves also tried to distract her. The old chiefs were more subtle. Their glances were casual. Any open sign of attraction could bring their wives down on them.

Kitsey had heard much of Chippewa ways during her capture. She knew that they came from Lake Millacs area and that the Mississippi above the falls of St. Anthony were much a Chippewa waterway. She could guess the plans Cass-Teo had for her, but why would he want Minnetaka?

The first day was continuous movement. Cass-Teo nibbled on dried meat and berries. He offered none. He spoke no word.

The young captives were free to speak, but said very little for fear of revealing their concern over their fate.

As the sun set, more than twenty-five miles had been covered. Tomorrow with the stream wider travel would be easier. Cass-Teo grunted in Chippewa, directing his words towards Kitsey. "Tomorrow he paddles also. Many miles."

That night Minnetaka was left to sleep, as best he could, in the canoe. The canoe was allowed to drift out in the current. Being bound hand and foot, escape was impossible and drowning always a danger. His concern was for Kitsey. He was able to see her, but unable to talk with her in private.

Kitsey was also tied hand and foot and so tightly the circulation was limited. She too was apprehensive about the coming night.

Cass-Teo offered her a tanned deer hide. It covered her well. He also had one for himself. He lay down facing Kitsey. She closed her eyes in fear. This cold face staring at her. If she could only sleep away this nightmare. Her mind went back to the previous night. How could the Great Spirit be so cruel to his children? Her eyes would not close. As the night deepened she could see less and less. Yet her eyes remained open. She wished for a sign that this face so near in the dark would soon emit sounds of heavy sleep. There was but soft deep breathing. Cass-Teo was not asleep.

Suddenly he whispered, "Are you sleeping?" She didn't answer. He whispered again, " Do you and your lover want to return to Red Wood? She didn't answer. I could let you both go in the morning." She was silent, but her pulse throbbed in her temple. He moved. It was his hand groping for her face. She recoiled in revulsion. As an animal she bit two of his fingers. He jerked, but she bit harder.

A fist came out of the dark and glanced off her forehead. As if by magic a desperate gamble entered her head. "I'm Chippewa, and proud of it, you snake! Red Iron is my uncle. My father was Chief Mesabi. If you touch me you'll be a eunuch the rest of your life!"

All was silent. Kitsey drew new courage from her tirade. Whatever she had said it served its purpose. She hoped Minnetaka in the canoe had heard it too. How she missed him. He was so close and yet so distant.

Minnetaka had spent the night in the canoe. Sleep was impossible. His eyes tried to penetrate the darkness, but he could see nothing. His ears strained for any sound. The quarrel made him full of fear and anger. He was amused at Kitsey's scolding. She had a spirit he admired. For a moment he too was convinced that she was daughter of a chief.

Minnetaka had wrestled with the problem of escape since his capture. There was no doubt that in any struggle Cass-Teo would certainly kill him. Even now there was a question as to why he kept him captive. It would seem so much easier without Minnetaka as another burden.

It was clear to Kitsey that she was to be a gift to a Chippewa chief. It was Cass-Teo's way to gain favor with the older chiefs.

From time to time Cass-Teo would be out of earshot. It gave Kitsey and Minnetaka a chance to talk.

"How far is it to the Mississippi?" asked Minnetaka.

Kitsey replied, "I don't know. It's a three and a half day journey. They speak of a falls at Portage Falls. We should reach there in two days. After that it's a half day to the Mississippi."

Minnetaka, "We must escape before reaching the Mississippi. The big river is in Chippewa country. If Cass-Teo heads upstream our chances of escape become very poor."

Kitsey, "There's another reason."

Minnetaka, "You mean _____?"

Kitsey, "Yes. Cass-Teo knew that we would choose to remain together rather than attempting to escape singley. Now that we are in Chippewa country he may feel that two prisoners are a greater risk than one. Your life is in danger. Cass-Teo will not hesitate. Your scalp at Kathio would call for a celebration. We must wait for our chance. My wrists are so tight that my fingers are numb."

Minnetaka said, "Wet the leather thongs as often as you can. Stumble in the water so they loosen a bit."

Kitsey, "The falls at Portage Falls lie ahead. It may be a chance to escape. I don't know the terrain. If Cass-Teo carries the canoe and if he frees our feet some chance may present itself."

Minnetaka, "Kitsey you are a brave girl. This day may be the most important day of our lives."

Kitsey, "Quiet, Cass-Teo is listening."

The second day dawned bright and sunny. The stream now a small river was high and moving fast. The miles passed quickly. The countryside was broken up by rolling hills of open prairie and vast groves of various hardwood trees. In the low areas were willow and poplar clumps and cattail bogs. At every turn of the river ducks of many varieties left the river. Mother teal were often seen leading their young to safety. Unable to fly, they followed in a perfect line behind the mother. It was a day to be enjoyed except for those without freedom.

As the trio approached the Portage Falls, Cass-Teo sent the canoe on to a narrow sandy landing. He grunted and motioned to Kitsey to crawl out. Being bound hand and foot it was awkward. Cass-Teo leaned over and loosened her ankle thongs. Minnetaka had been paddling so was free to use his hands. But Cass-Teo was taking no chances. He loosened the ankle thongs allowing them to walk, but only in short half steps. As a further precaution, he tied another leather rope to a high overhanging limb. Then Cass-Teo, swinging the canoe on his shoulder, turned and said, "Don't move. I want your scalps." He moved swiftly down the portage into a low area that was dense with swamp willows. He never returned.

The Sioux at Medayto were reluctant to leave. It was summer. Time was no problem. Food, especially fish, were close at hand. They had succeeded in freeing the Kandiyohi Lake region from the Chippewas. One by one they headed for the open prairies that would take them to their homes.

Kiyi, after enjoying his first victory, was ready to return home. There were others his age ready and mounted. Young braves, proud of their mounts, would cover the fifty miles in two days or less.

As they approached the familiar bluff that lines the Minnesota River Valley, women and children ran to meet them. It was the first news of the battle. The young braves had not anticipated such a conquering hero's reception.

Kiyi reined his horse out from the crowd and sought a narrow washout trail that descended into a wooded ravine. It took him to the lodge of his parents. His father was following with the older warriors. But first Kiyi must tell Tya about her grandson, Minnetaka.

Tya as always was moving between fire and teepee. Every year a little slower. She seemed eternally intent on the ground ahead of her. It was her back -it bent more every year.

As Kiyi approached, his shadow fell across her path. She looked up squinting in the bright sun. She knew his name, but merely grunted. She waved one arm weakly. It was her offer of food. She again stood stooped and silent. It was her invitation to Kiyi to speak.

Kiyi, not knowing where to start blurted out, "Minnetaka found Kitsey. We saw their tracks in the sand. But they are gone. We saw more tracks. Tracks of three people. It was by the Medayto outlet. No more tracks, they must be going by canoe."

21
The Rescue

Tya looked up. There was a spark in her small black eyes. "Chippewa territory," she muttered. "Ghost Weasel, the trapper, knows the river. Go to his lodge and tell him to come," she continued.

Kiyi went directly to the lodge of Ghost Weasel. He was old, but had never wanted the problems of leadership. He preferred trapping and hunting usually alone, but often with younger men eager to learn his skills. In the years that Sioux occupied the Kandiyohi Lakes he had the opportunity to become acquainted with lakes and rivers for many miles in each direction.

"Come to Tya's," said Kiyi. "Minnetaka has been captured. Maybe now in Chippewa territory, by canoe, on the Karishon. Do you know the river?"

Ghost Weasel replied, "I change, but the river doesn't change. It has been many years. What are your plans?"

"We are planning on catching them before they reach the big river. There will be three of us. Tell us a good place to wait for them. We must surprise their captors. We will leave yet today. With good horses we can be there in a day and a half," said Kiyi.

"Look for a portage at Portage Falls. It goes through low wet ground dense with swamp willows. It's the best chance. Be like shadows," counselled Ghost Weasel.

Kiyi called to his friends who were standing nearby. "Weasel and Yellow Bee, will you ride with me? It will be a test of our stealth if we succeed in finding them. We need food for five days. Meet me here as soon as you have talked with your family. I am going to the chief for permission. Bring Blackie and one extra horse. Tya, I am hungry, what are you preparing?"

Tya moved with new vigor, hobbling to her lodge she produced dried venison and corn bread. In separate leather pouches she packed dried berries, cracked corn, squash seeds and honey mixed with a variety of nuts.

When Kiyi had finished she showed him a soft leather ball with a dozen bird feathers. There were colors from the flicker, the blue jay, and the white gull. Kiyi puzzled over it. Tya noticed and spoke softly. "The Great Spirit hears me when I pray. This medicine puff will protect you. It will bring all of you safely back to me." She put it in his strong hand and patted it warmly. The blue veins protruded from the back of her withered hand. The hand with the finger stubs.

Getting permission was not easy. The highest ranking chiefs were still in the Kandiyohi Lakes area. The young braves were untested in battle, and not well acquainted in the area they were entering. Permission was granted because time was so important. Minnetaka was a well respected young brave, and Kitsey had become well known because she had been taken from the Sioux earlier in the summer. It was a matter of honor that the tribe make an effort for their release.

Starting while the sun was still high the trio plus two extra horses headed up the bluffs and then followed a course northeast. At Hutchinson they reached the South Fork of the Crow River. A small group of Winnebago Sioux were camped there. From them they were given directions to Portage Falls by the way of the South Fork of the Crow.

The trio moved as daylight permitted, stopping only when darkness prevented their traveling. One of the trio was always far ahead as a scout. The second rider with the extra horses kept him in sight at all times. The third rider rode to the rear as a guard. They were in Sioux territory, but danger was always present. In another day they would be at Portage Falls. If they were lucky they would intercept the captor and his captives there.

Kiyi and his chosen friends had found the Portage Falls portage. The dense swamp willows were ideal for an ambush. At the end of the portage they found the sand bar that Ghost Weasel had mentioned. The thick willows cast deep shadows. Kiyi placed himself nearest the center of the sand bar. The other young warriors were on his flanks. They had planned with care this fatal ambush. Cass-Teo was a huge, dangerous hunter and warrior. If he escaped, though wounded, he would surely try to kill his prisoners. There had been no new tracks in the muddy portage. It meant Cass-Teo was still coming their way. It was agreed that all would shoot in unison at close range. They waited in the dense willows. Their wait was not long.

Cass-Teo was pushing to reach the Mississippi. He made sure his prisoners were well tied. Now he must carry the canoe through the swampy portage, and return to bring his hobbled captives. As he walked, the canoe above him caught in over-hanging branches. The trail, though well traveled, was filled with roots and pockets of mud.

Upon reaching the narrow bank of sand at the river's edge, he was about to unload the heavy burden. He turned the canoe over, letting it down to the ground slowly. Both arms were holding the canoe. It was at this

The Ambush

moment that he saw the hate of the Sioux for the Chippewas and this Chippewa in particular.

The arrows came from three directions. At close range some passed through the soft flesh of the belly. Several penetrated the rib cage. The internal bleeding would bring death quickly.

But Cass-Teo had fought before. He bounded towards Kiyi with tomahawk upraised and with a wild scream. But the scream was never finished and the tomahawk never landed.

He pitched forward on his face sending some arrows deeper into his body. As the three watched, they saw the blood and pink froth gurgle from his nose and mouth with each heavy breath. Oblivious of his killers, now his life was reduced to a few muscle twitches. Soon he lay still. The huge man was dead.

It was Cass-Teo's scream that alerted Minnetaka and Kitsey. It was violence and close at hand. They were helpless. They could not defend themselves. They could not run. Their ears and eyes strained for more information. Out of the shaded swamp willows they saw movement. It was more than one person. Yes, there were three coming toward them. The three figures moved quietly - cautiously.

Minnetaka was the first to speak - he tried to control his voice. He offered a question with an answer. "Kiyi?" Yes, it was Kiyi. "And here is Weasel and Yellow Bee. Kitsey come." Kitsey came forward. In a grave voice and with an earnest face she said, "you have saved our lives, by risking your own. How can we ever repay you?"

Kiyi spoke, "We have brought Blackie and another horse for Kitsey. We are not safe here. If we ride down the river until dark, we will be near the Big Falls. From there we must go southwest across the prairie. Our friends, the Winnebagoes, are a day's journey. We could be there by sundown tomorrow."

Minnetaka spoke, "We must conceal the body of Cass-Teo. Together we can drag him over the hill away from the river. Our tracks along the river could alert a passing Chippewa."

Kiyi added, "There is the canoe, what shall we do with it?"

Weasel spoke, "Let's hide it deep in these swamp willows. Anyone finding it will think its owner hid it."

Minnetaka had another idea, "It's an excellent canoe, better than most of ours. If we could reach the Big Falls no one would question our ownership."

Kitsey spoke, "How do we dare to travel on the big river in a Chippewa canoe? Certainly someone would suspect us."

Minnetaka replied, "We could follow the shore with the horses. I would be alone in the canoe. If danger appears I will come ashore. Once on horses we would be able to outrun our pursuers."

Kitsey raised her voice, "Is the canoe worth all the risk? We're safe. I think we should go home to our valley."

22
The Mississippi

Minnetaka spoke in reply, "Kitsey, you said your mother lived on the big river. She must think of you. Does she know what has happened to you? Do you want to see her?"

Kitsey was caught off guard. She hadn't thought of her mother often. The only word she heard was when traders along the Minnesota would carry word of her. Usually the information was vague. Her mother, though Chippewa, had lived with a Sioux on the Sibley Island below the great bluff. "I would like to see my mother. I have a sister also. But the danger in going down river is real. I won't ask you to take such a chance."

Minnetaka looked at his rescuers. "If we hug the shore and travel after dark, we could get the canoe to the Big Falls. We could be there by morning."

St. Anthony Falls

COMMENTARY

The present Minneapolis-St. Paul area is divided by the Mississippi River. The Mississippi River comes from the north, making a large S curve before continuing southward. The Minnesota joins it from the west. At present day Fort Snelling, smaller rivers like the St. Croix, Elk River, Rum River and the combined Crow Rivers attract Indian commerce up to 200 miles in each direction. It was as often a battleground as it was neutral ground. Tribes found that by observing the neutrality of the region they could barter their surpluses in exchange for items not found in their local regions.

The Mississippi above St. Cloud was exclusively a Chippewa waterway. It led north to all their many settlements. In the shape of a giant question mark, it began at Lake Itasca several hundred miles to the north. It then flows through Lake Bemidji, Cass Lake, Lake Winnibigoshish to Grand Rapids, Aitkin, Brainerd, and St. Cloud. The Crow Wing chain of lakes led to the big Leech Lake encampments. The Rum River and a series of small lakes and portages led to Lake Millacs. The main Chippewa camp was Kathio, site of the historic defeat of the Sioux.

The Falls of St. Anthony (the Big Falls) in downtown Minneapolis are created by water flowing over the hard underlying granite escarpment. Below the falls is a channel of soft limestone with nearly vertical sides. The habitable areas were restricted to the few areas that sloped gently to the river. These areas are Fort Snelling, downtown St. Paul and Sibley Island.

Trade, while limited between tribes, was carried on almost out of necessity. Here the Chippewas would exchange their wild rice, fish, furs and blueberries for corn, dried buffalo meat, and nuts. Horses, canoes and copper tools were also items of barter. Traders from many tribes would come to the area with the understanding that organized tribal clashes would be counter productive.

The Big Falls were an attraction for children. They had heard it described; for its shimmering beauty, for its huge rocks, and for its tremendous roar as its clear water tumbled thirty feet into a white mist.

It was agreed. The opportunity to see the falls met with approval of Weasel, Yellow Bee, and Kiyi. Kitsey was reluctant, but the thought of seeing her mother made her agree.

Again they moved with a scout ahead and a rear guard. Kitsey chose to go with Minnetaka in the canoe. With two paddling the time would be less.

A well worn path paralleled the river, but there were many detours around low bog areas and dense thickets of wild plum, sumac, and cedars. Keeping in contact became a real problem until the moon became high. From then on the canoe moved in its silvery reflection.

Minnetaka, "Kitsey, it is the same moon."

Kitsey, "Yes, I remember. It is our moon. Could the Great Spirit tell us of our future? Do you pray to the Great Spirit, Minnetaka?"

Minnetaka, "I pray every morning as I greet the day. I stand in the doorway of the lodge and face the rising sun. I ask for another day. Every day he answers - he gives me another day. He has never failed me."

Kitsey, "But did you pray this morning? Were you so certain that he would give you a new day today?"

Minnetaka, "No. Cass-Teo convinced me that this would be my last day."

Kitsey, "I, too, expected him to kill you. We had no chance to free ourselves and escape. Was Kiyi sent by the Great Spirit?"

Minnetaka, "I think Kiyi had the idea, and the Great Spirit protected him from harm."

Kitsey, "I hear the sound of the falls. Paddle towards shore. We can camp nearby and wait for daylight. It seems to be getting light in the east. It will be a short night."

Up at first light, Minnetaka stretched his legs by rising on his toes. His muscled thighs tightened. He inhaled deeply. Closing his eyes and looking upward he thanked the Great Spirit for his and Kitsey's delivery from their captor the day before.

Kitsey remained asleep. Minnetaka studied her pleasant face. He watched her even breathing. How fortunate am I that she is mine. She stirred and in a lazy voice murmured, "I could sleep a whole day."

Minnetaka, "The boys are still asleep, but we must wake them and move on."

Kitsey, "Wait, let them sleep. Come with me. A quick swim will wake us."

Together they ran to the water's edge and plunged in. Minnetaka came up first. He waited for her to appear. She swam underwater to appear behind him, sinking him in a single motion. He responded and found her moving along the rocky bottom. It was an endurance contest. He soon overtook her and they rose together gasping for air. The short swim over, they returned to shore.

The sound of the falls beckoned. At a distance all one heard was a continuous low rumble. As one approached the falls the rumble became a roar. As one listened it was as if the falls were grumbling.

Kitsey crawled over giant sections of jagged rock below the falls. The mist wet her face as if in a rain shower. Suddenly she called to the others.

"Do you hear her?" The sound of her voice was lost in the rumble of the falls. Upon coming closer she again asked, "Do you hear her?"

In unison they asked, "Hear who?"

"The maiden in the falls," Kitsey replied. "You can hear her if you listen carefully. She was promised by her father to a mean chief. But she was in love with a young brave. The chief, when he found out, sent the young warrior on a dangerous mission. He was killed. When the maiden learned of his death, she took a canoe and went over the falls singing her song. It's the same song that she sings today. Young lovers can even make out the sad words she sings. Do you hear her, Minnetaka?"

"Yes, I hear her," he replied.

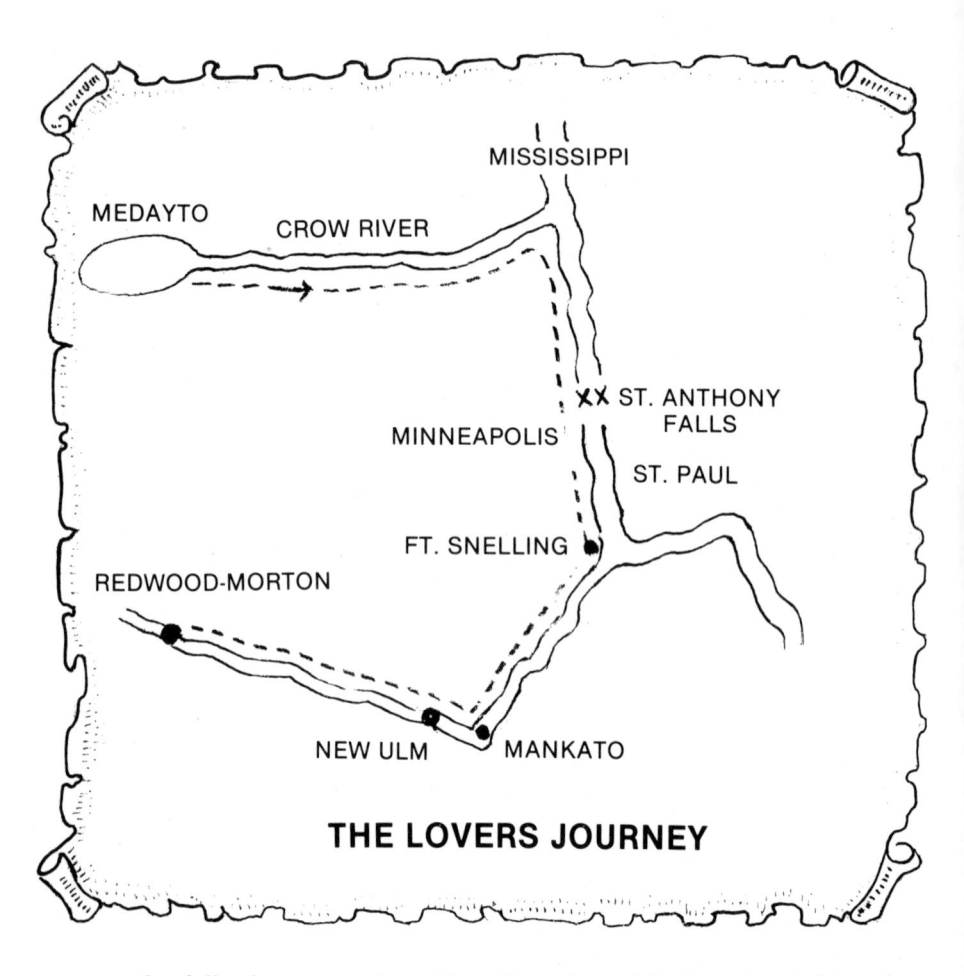

THE LOVERS JOURNEY

At the falls they separated. Kiyi, Weasel, and Yellow Bee taking the horses headed overland to the Minnesota River Valley. Kitsey and Minnetaka had chosen to go by the way of the Minnesota River to the Red Wood Falls encampment. This would give them the time to search for

Kitsey's mother and sister.

Five miles below the falls they found a low island with many teepees. It was at the joining of the Mississippi and the Minnesota Rivers. It was called Traders Island. Across the river was the Great Bluff or High Meadow. It commanded a view of all river traffic from the three directions. It was a neutral meeting place for trade and travel. The white men would some day call it Fort Snelling.

Kitsey and Minnetaka landed on the Traders Island below the great bluff. Kitsey asked the few that greeted their arrival if they knew Red Bird. No one seemed to know of her. Then Kitsey remembered that she had taken a Sioux name, it was a nickname, Happy Swallow. Yes, they knew her. She lives up on the bluff in the summer and on the island during the winter.

It was a long gradual climb to the top of the great bluff. Every step improved the view of the rivers. The bottom lands of the Minnesota contained lakes and ponds as far as the eye could see.

Once on top of the bluff they were confronted with a wide level prairie, with clusters of lodges in every direction. The Indians were mostly Sioux and smaller tribes friendly to both the Sioux and the Chippewas.

Kitsey, after inquiry, was directed to her mother's lodge. It was a big cone-shaped teepee. Its sides were lifted to allow free flow of air. Everything was neat and clean.

Kitsey approached the teepee and called her mother's name. There was a growl from within. After calling again a tall man appeared at the opening. He said nothing, but waited for Kitsey to speak.

Kitsey offered, "I'm looking for a woman called Happy Swallow. Is she here? I'm her daughter."

The man replied, "She is fishing west of here. She will return soon."

He was a Sioux by his tall lean figure and bony facial features. He was in no hurry to communicate, but finally asked, "Did you come by way of the Minnesota Valley trail?"

Minnetaka replied, "We came by canoe, from above the Big Falls."

His manner changed, "Chippewa territory that direction. Why did you choose that area?"

Minnetaka responded, "It was not our choice. We were prisoners. Cass-Teo wanted revenge."

"I know of Cass-Teo. A bad Indian. But for what revenge?"

"Haven't you heard that the Sioux drove the Chippewas out of the Kandiyohi Lakes just a few days ago?"

The big Indian was eager for more information. "Who were the chiefs? Tell me about the battle. How many warriors? How many killed?" Looking far away he said as if to himself, "It will not end next year or the year after, the war will continue. Living here has been safe, but who knows when the battle will spread."

23
The Wedding Celebration

Across the meadow a woman leading a black and white horse appeared. A young colt with similar markings trotted awkwardly at her side. As the group approached the woman broke into a broad smile and said, "It's my little White Swan. Let me look at you. How you have grown!"

Happy Swallow was excited. "Have you come to visit? You must stay with us. We need time to talk. Your sister lives nearby."

"Hoky, take the mare. We will eat fish tonight. Hoky, this is my daughter, White Swan."

Kitsey replied, "Hoky, this is Minnetaka. We want you and mother to bless our marriage."

Happy Swallow answered in a high voice, "We will have a wedding celebration. In two days all will be ready."

The next two days were busy days for mother and daughter. Many women offered help with cooking, baking, sewing and cleaning. Younger girls were running errands, fetching water and taking care of younger children. A wedding was an event that brought out the older squaws. The ceremony would be brief, but the preparation would take two days.

Minnetaka and Hoky escaped the confusion by going downstream searching for large snapping turtles. Finding the river turtle was easy, but catching them once they dove under the water required great perseverence. If the turtle sought clear water a strong underwater swimmer could see them and overtake them. But a turtle bent on escape rarely surfaced until well beyond his pursuers. The time spent hunting turtles was pleasant. The cleaning of the turtles was more of a problem. The celebration would feature turtle stews. There would be several types, because the turtle has meats with various tastes.

The second day Minnetaka and Hoky went by horseback to the lake of many bays. The Sioux called it Minne-Tonka. Hoky said the Indians at Minne-Tonka were friendly and had huge northern pike for barter. Hoky had traded a canoe for several copper spearheads. Fish spears were much prized by all Indians. He was sure they would offer a half dozen big pike in exchange.

Minnetaka was struck by the beauty of the large lake with its islands, wooded points, channels and white sand beaches. He wished Kitsey would have shared the experience. Maybe in the future they would return together.

The day of the wedding celebration dawned clear and bright. Minnetaka watched the wedding preparation with mixed emotions. He and Kitsey would be more than lovers. They would now be man and wife. Always in his mind, his love and respect for Kitsey was something that deserved expression. The wedding was just such a celebration. There would be music, dancing, chanting, all in high spirits. It was meant to tease and embarrass the young couple. It also united the guests into a friendly festival mood. Food was everywhere. It was as if the settlement had been waiting for an excuse for a celebration.

Two of the older women were experienced in organizing the mock courtship. Kitsey was given a teepee and an adopted family to go with it. She remained in her teepee as several suitors made a bid for her hand by presenting themselves at the door of her teepee. Each offered a dowry, each was turned down by her appointed father. Small children grinned and taunted the suitors. The young braves jeered at the disappointed suitors.

Then Minnetaka appeared and stood beside her teepee. He was leading a black and white colt. No one came out from the teepee. It was embarrassing to Minnetaka, but the guests knew of the outcome and enjoyed his

Minnetaka Courts his Kitsey

discomfort. Meanwhile braves offered additional items in jest to Minnetaka. He refused them, but again the crowd taunted him as being unworthy of Kitsey.

Soon the mother came out muttering to herself that her husband was too greedy and that he should accept Minnetaka's dowry which was the colt. The crowd showed their agreement. At this she looks up and grins a toothless grin and goes in the teepee again. This time there is much argument in the teepee. The old squaw is pleading on Kitsey's behalf. Meanwhile Minnetaka stands alone holding the rein of the colt.

Finally the old couple appeared. The old man took the colt's lead rope and studied the colt carefully. Satisfied that the colt is sound, he waves to the older men and they cheer his acceptance. The old man handed the lead rope to the old squaw to care for and he gave the colt a slap on the rump. He then disappeared inside the teepee. Kitsey was now ready, with the help of three women in attendance, to come out and accept Minnetaka as her husband.

Kitsey appeared in a long near white buckskin tunic that reached her knees. It was a beautiful pattern of beads, rich dye colors and symbolic designs. The neck was beaded. The hem was fringed with white weasel tails hanging below the fringe. Her skin was smooth with a satin oil lustre. Her black eyes sparkled within the frame formed by two hair braids that hung down the front of her buckskin tunic. Her moccasins were light tan, likely from the belly skin of a young elk. They too were fine samples of decorative art. All items were on loan for this occasion. They were kept for such occasions. It became an honor for the woman who had done the fine ornamentation.

Minnetaka, tall and handsome, was a matched opposite of Kitsey in that he was without adornments. His hair was glossy with oil. A narrow headband held a single eagle feather, a gift from Hoky. His new moccasins were a gift from Happy Swallow.

Kitsey, attended by the three older squaws, was slow about emerging from the wigwam. As she appeared she wore a slight smile. Evidently one of the squaws had a last word for her.

She approached Minnetaka. He swung open his arm that held his blanket. As Kitsey moved close to him she saw how tense he was. It made her smile. Finally he wrapped his blanket around her. The two embraced behind the blanket as the guests roared approval. They retired to a teepee provided. There they were alone for several hours. The guests were already starting to dance and eat. Kitsey and Minnetaka would be honored as the evening approached.

The wedding celebration started at dusk. Food was again served. It was supplied by guests and others who came as well-wishers. The crowd increased as the drummers gathered. What started as three drums soon became eight or ten drums. The rhythm inspired the very old as well as the small children. Some of the drums accompanied a singer whose song had words that all understood. It was more chant than song. It spoke of the virtues of a good woman.

The dancers followed the drum lead, but at times the younger boys and warriors would improvise by calling like a certain animal. Sometimes it was as if they were answering an invisible person in the sky. The effect was to ignite passion of the dancers. Soon all were calling out their own narrative. It produced an exciting jamboree.

The crowd called on Minnetaka to join the dance. Minnetaka begged off, but Kitsey insisted. Minnetaka had wanted to learn to dance. The occasion simply had not arisen. The dance was for men only. Women kept time with their feet on the sidelines. Minnetaka started slowly. His legs were of wood. It seemed simple, shuffle one foot, then hop. Repeat on the other foot. It was as if his legs were dead. By watching others he saw how perfectly these simple foot movements were tied to the beat of the drums. By listening more and looking at his feet less he soon fell into the rhythm. In a short time he, too, was feeling a release. The drum beat, the dance, and the whirling bodies helped him express his strength, his youth, his happiness.

Kitsey, honored guest, was the object of much curiosity and admiration. The hundreds of women living on the High Meadow gave her gifts and much advice. Tomorrow would be a strenuous day on the river.

24
The Homecoming

The following morning Minnetaka and Kitsey were ready for their journey. Happy Swallow and Hoky had filled a parafleche with dried berries, dried fish, honey and nuts. There were gifts of pottery, tanned furs and a beautifully decorated soft deer hide dress.

Paddling up the Minnesota was quite different. The current was sluggish, but to overcome it made travel slower.

Kitsey said, "We have time. This beautiful river scenery requires patience to be enjoyed. It seems, Minnetaka, that the birds sing just for us. The beaver and muskrats seem not to fear us. Up there, a kingfisher waits as we approach. Then look! He dives from his perch, screaming as he sweeps near the water, then in a continuation of the dive finds another high perch, this time just behind us."

As they approached the Mankato area, the bluffs along the river showed a tan limestone named after a Sioux Chief called Kasota. The soft stone had been cut away to make caves by tribes who lived here long before anyone could remember.

Some tribes used the caves as part of a winter dwelling. It's even inside temperature was better than the bitter cold of Minnesota winters.

Other tribes considered them as haunted by bad spirits, believing the dead still occupied the deep recesses.

Minnetaka, always respectful of the dead and bad spirits, kept silent.

Friendly Sioux tribes were scattered along the river. The Wanamingoes, and the Winnebagoes, as well as the Santee called this part of their river, home. Frequently they would hail the canoe as it passed. More than once their conversation carried across the quiet stream. The design of the canoe marked it as a Chippewa product.

Leaving Mankato behind, the two voyageurs were on the last leg of their journey. Friendly Sioux from the Morton camps would appear. Their curiousity turned to enthusiastic greeting when they realized this was the two who were captured. Kiyi and his friends had spread the word of their rescue and their return by canoe from the Big Falls.

At the Red Wood-Morton Camp all able bodied were on the banks awaiting their arrival. Young boys swam to meet them. Older boys waded out to guide their canoe to shore. The well wishers surrounded the pair as they left the river and crossed the meadow toward their lodges.

Minnetaka looked for Tya. She would be waiting. But first the chiefs greeted the pair. Then the women surrounded Kitsey to hear her story of the capture, the rescue and the wedding celebration.

Minnetaka raised his arms requesting the opportunity to be heard. "Hear me brothers. I have been no hero. I and Kitsey draw breath today because of my three courageous friends, Kiyi, Weasel, and Yellow Bee. They have counted coup. They must be heard at the council fires."

Minnetaka broke away to seek out Tya. She was nowhere to be seen. He entered her lodge. She was sitting facing the entrance. She seemed smaller.

Minnetaka approached her. She looked up. She was breathing hard. She spoke hoarsely. He leaned over to hear. "You are back. I am glad. You now have a woman. That is good." She paused for breath and studied Kitsey. "Soon you will have a baby - life will go on. When the snow of spring is gone, I too, will be gone."

"Tya, no. You must live to enjoy your great grandchild. My woman will make you warm and well fed, Tya. The baby, if a girl, will carry your name 'Little Tya.' If it is a boy he will be called, like his great grandfather - 'Little Crow.' "

OLD TYA SINGS

The birds leave, the snowflakes follow.
The long night of the winter aches the bones.
Winter snows will vanish, Spring will come,
But Tya will not greet the robin's return.

Blow winds of the winter prairie.
Let the daylight become dark and let the
northern sky move as a ghostly curtain of light.

Let me exchange these tired hands for the
body and mind of my youth.
Let me step beyond that curtain of light to
greet those who beckon to me from afar.

Youth follows the aged.
The new are born - memories become myths.
Myths become dreams, all is the same. The
past is today and I welcome the new dawn.

The birds leave, the snowflakes follow.
The long night of the winter aches the bones.
Winter snows will vanish, Spring will come,
But Tya will not greet the robin's return.

J.G.B.

Printed by:
MARACOM/COLOR PRESS, WILLMAR, MINNESOTA

The author-artist is a Willmar native who lived and studied art in Washington, D.C., served in the Army as an artist in London and Paris. He returned to Willmar to follow a variety of interests that include art, writing, advertising, land development and farming.

Other Books by J. Gordon Bergquist

"Summer Boy", a nostalgic reminder of farm life during the 1920's.

"Once A Boy", scenes of his boyhood as he grew up in Willmar, Minnesota.

Order Form

Price Increase

Now includes tax

Title	Qty.	Price	Total
Minnetaka Indian Boy		9.75	
Summer Boy		4.25	
Once A Boy		4.25	
(Add 75¢ Postage for each)		**TOTAL**	

Name _____

Address _____

City _____

State _____ Zip _____

Bergquist Publishing

4652

414 West Seventh Street
Willmar, Minnesota 56201
(612) 235-4516